PENGUIN MODERN CLASSICS

Over to Candleford

Flora Jane Thompson was born in 1876 at Juniper Hill, a hamlet on the borders of Oxfordshire and Northamptonshire. After leaving school she was sent as assistant to the postmistress (who also kept the forge) to a town eight miles away, and was for some time employed to carry the letters in a locked leather bag to the big house nearby. So began her long connection with the Post Office. She married young and her husband later became a postmaster. His work took them to Bournemouth, where she obtained from the public library the Greek and Roman classics in translation, as well as Ibsen and the English poets, novelists and critics – especially Shaw and Yeats. Her first book was a collection of poems, *Bog Myrtle and Peat*. However, she is best remembered for three auto-biographical volumes: *Lark Rise* (1939), *Over to Candleford* (1941) and *Candleford Green* (1943), reissued in one volume as *Lark Rise to Candleford* (1945). A fourth volume, *Still Glides the Stream*, was published posthumously in 1948. Flora Thompson died at Brixham, Devon, on 21 May 1947.

FLORA THOMPSON

Over to Candleford

PENGUIN BOOKS

PENGUIN CLASSICS

Published by the Penguin Group
Penguin Books Ltd, 80 Strand, London WC2R ORL, England
Penguin Group (USA) Inc., 375 Hudson Street, New York, New York 10014, USA
Penguin Group (Canada), 90 Eglinton Avenue East, Suite 700, Toronto, Ontario, Canada M4P 2Y3
(a division of Pearson Penguin Canada Inc.)
Penguin Ireland, 25 St Stephen's Green, Dublin 2, Ireland
(a division of Penguin Books Ltd)
Penguin Group (Australia), 250 Camberwell Road, Camberwell, Victoria 3124, Australia
(a division of Pearson Australia Group Pty Ltd)
Penguin Books India Pvt Ltd, 11 Community Centre, Panchsheel Park, New Delhi – 110 017, India
Penguin Group (NZ), 67 Apollo Drive, Rosedale, North Shore 0632, New Zealand
(a division of Pearson New Zealand Ltd)
Penguin Books (South Africa) (Pty) Ltd, 24 Sturdee Avenue, Rosebank, Johannesburg 2196, South Africa

Penguin Books Ltd, Registered Offices: 80 Strand, London WC2R ORL, England

www.penguin.com

First published by Oxford University Press 1941
Published in Penguin Classics 2009
This film and TV tie-in edition published 2009
By arrangement with the BBC
BBC © BBC 1996
The BBC logo is a registered trademark of the
British Broadcasting Corporation and is used under license.
1

Copyright © Flora Thompson, 1941
All rights reserved

Set in 10.5/13 pt PostScript Monotype Dante
Typeset by Rowland Phototypesetting Ltd, Bury St Edmunds, Suffolk
Printed in England by Clays Ltd, St Ives plc

978-0-141-19015-0

www.greenpenguin.co.uk

Contents

I

As They Were

'Come the summer, we'll borrow old Polly and the spring cart from the "Wagon and Horses" and all go over to Candleford,' their father said, for the ten-millionth time, thought Laura. Although he had said it so often they had never been. They had not been anywhere farther than the market town for the Saturday shopping.

Once, when some one asked them how long they had lived in their cottage, Laura had replied, 'Oh, for years and years,' and Edmund had said 'Always'; but his always was only five years and her years and years were barely seven. That was why, when their mother told them that the greatest mistake in life is to be born poor, they did not realize that they themselves had made that initial blunder. They were too young and had no means of comparison.

Their home was one of a group of small cottages surrounded by fields, three miles from the nearest small town and nineteen from a city. All around was rich, flat farming country, which, at the end of a lifetime, remained obstinately in the memory as stretch after stretch of brown-ribbed ploughland patterned with quick-set hedges and hedgerow elms. That picture was permanent; others could be called up at will, of acres of young green wheat swept by chasing cloud-shadows; of the gold of harvest fields, or the billowing white-ness of snow upon which the spoor of hares and foxes could be traced from hedgerow to hedgerow.

On a slight rise in the midst of this brown or green or whiteness stood the hamlet, a huddle of grey stone walls and pale slated roofs with only the bushiness of a fruit-tree or the dark line of a yew hedge to relieve its colourlessness. To a passer-by on the main road a mile away it must often have appeared a lone and desolate place;

but it had a warmth of its own, and a closer observer would have found it as seething with interest and activity as a molehill.

All the cottages in the group were occupied by poor families. Some, through old age, or the possession of a larger family than ordinary, had a little less, and two or three in more favourable circumstances had a little more comfort than their neighbours, but in every house money was scarce.

If any one wanted to borrow, they knew better than to ask for more than sixpence, and if the expression with which their request was received was discouraging they would add hurriedly: 'If you can't manage it, I think tuppence'd see me through.' The children were given halfpennies or even farthings to spend on sweets when the travelling grocer's van called. For even the smaller sum they got enough hardbake or peppermint rock to distend their cheeks for hours. It took the parents months to save up to buy a young pig for the sty or a few score of faggots for the winter. Apart from the prudent, who had these small hoards, people were penniless for days towards the end of the week.

But, as they were fond of saying, money isn't everything. Poor as they were, every one of the small cottages, so much alike when seen from the outside, had for its inmates the unique distinction of being 'our place' or 'ho-um'. After working in the pure cold air of the fields all day, the men found it comforting to be met by, and wrapped round in, an atmosphere of chimney-smoke and bacon and cabbage-cooking; to sink into 'feyther's chair' by the hearth, draw off heavy, mud-caked boots, take the latest baby on their knee and sip strong, sweet tea while 'our Mum' dished up the tea-supper.

The elder children were either at school all day or lived out of doors in fine weather; but, as their mothers said, they knew which house to go to when they felt hungry, and towards dusk they made for their supper and bed like homing pigeons, or rabbits scurrying to their burrows.

To the women, home was home in a special sense, for nine-tenths of their lives were spent indoors. There they washed and cooked and cleaned and mended for their teeming families; there they enjoyed their precious half-hour's peace with a cup of tea before the fire in the afternoon, and there they bore their troubles as best they could and cherished their few joys. At times when things did not press too heavily upon them they found pleasure in re-arranging their few poor articles of furniture, in re-papering the walls and making quilts and cushions of scraps of old cloth to adorn their dwelling and add to its comfort, and few were so poor that they had not some treasure to exhibit, some article that had been in the family since 'I dunno when', or had been bought at a sale of furniture at such-and-such a great house, or had been given them when in service.

Such treasures in time gained a reputation of fabulous value. Bill's grandfather had refused an offer of twenty pounds for that corner cupboard, or grandfather's clock, said one; another that a mysterious gentleman had once told her that the immense rubies and emeralds which studded a shabby old metal photograph frame were real stones. She was always saying that she would take it to a jeweller at Sherston and get it valued, 'come Fair time', but she never did. Like the rest of us, she knew better than to put her favourite illusion to the test.

None of the listeners cast doubt upon the value of such treasures. It would not have been 'manners', and, besides, nearly everybody had got some article with a similar legend. At home, the children's father laughed and said that as none of the Braby family had ever had more than twenty shillings at one time in their lives an offer of twenty pounds would soon have been snapped at; and as to Mrs Gaskin's rubies and emeralds, anybody with half an eye could see that they came from the same mine as the stuff used to make penny tumblers.

'What's the odds, if thinking so makes them happy?' asked his wife.

They were a hardworking, self-reliant, passably honest people. 'Providence helps them as has got the sense to look out for theirselves' was a motto often quoted. They had not much original wit, but had inherited a stock of cheerful sayings which passed as such. A neighbour called in to help move a heavy piece of furniture would arrive spitting on his palms and saying, 'Here I be, ready an' willin'' to do as much for half a crown as I 'ud for a shillin'.' Which mild joke, besides the jumbled arithmetic, had the added point of the fantastic sum suggested as a reward. A glass of beer, or the price of one, was the current payment for that and some more considerable services.

One who had helped a neighbour to solve some knotty problem would quote the old proverb: 'Two heads be better n'r one,' and the other would retort, 'That's why fools get married,' or, if materially minded, 'Aye, specially if 'um be sheep's heads.' A proverb always had to be capped. No one could say, 'There's more ways of killing a dog than hanging it' without being reminded, 'nor of choking it with a pound of fresh butter', and any reference to money as the root of all evil would be followed, by, 'Same time, I 'udn't say no to anybody as offered me a slip off that root.'

The discussion of their own and their neighbours' affairs took the place occupied by books and films in the modern outlook. Nothing of outside importance ever happened there and their lives were as unlike as possible the modern conception of country life, for Lark Rise was neither a little hotbed of vice nor a garden of all the Arcadian virtues. But the lives of all human beings, however narrow, have room for complications for themselves and entertainment for the onlooker, and many a satisfying little drama was played out on that ten-foot stage.

In their daily life they had none of the conveniences now looked upon as necessities: no water nearer than the communal well, no sanitation beyond the garden closet, and no light but candles and paraffin lamps. It was a hard life, but the hamlet folks did not pity themselves. They kept their pity for those they thought really poor.

The children brought home from the Sunday School Lending Library books about the London slums which their mothers also read. This was then a favourite subject with writers of that class of fiction; their object apparently being not so much to arouse indignation at the terrible conditions as to provide a striking background for some ministering lady or child. Many tears were shed in the hamlet over *Christie's Old Organ* and *Froggy's Little Brother*, and everybody wished they could have brought those poor neglected slum children there and shared with them the best they had of everything. 'Poor little mite. If we could have got him here, he could have slept with our young Sammy and this air'd have set him up in no time,' one woman said of Froggy's poor dying little brother, forgetting that he was, as she would have said at another time, 'just somebody in a book'.

But, saddening as it was to read about the poor things, it was also enjoyable, for it gave one a cheering sense of superiority. Thank God, the reader had a whole house to herself with an upstairs and downstairs and did not have to 'pig it' in one room; and real beds, and clean ones, not bundles of rags in corners, to sleep on.

To them, as to the two children learning to live among them, the hamlet life was the normal life. On one side of that norm were the real poor, living in slums, and, on the other, 'the gentry'. They recognized no other division of classes; although, of course, they knew there were a few 'bettermost people' between. The visiting clergyman and that kind friend of them all, the doctor in the market town, had more money and better houses than theirs, and though they were both 'gentlemen born' they did not belong to the aristocracy inhabiting the great country houses or visiting the hunting boxes around. But these were, indulgently, 'th' ole parson', and, affectionately, 'our doctor'; they were not thought of as belonging to any particular class of society.

The gentry flitted across the scene like kingfishers crossing a flock of hedgerow sparrows. They saw them sweeping through the hamlet in their carriages, the ladies billowing in silks and satins, with tiny chenille-fringed parasols held at an angle to protect their complexions. Or riding to hounds in winter, the men in immaculate pink, the women sitting their side-saddles with hour-glass figures encased in skin-tight black habits. *'Looks for all the world as if she'd been melted and poured into it, now don't she?'* On raw, misty mornings they would trot their horses through on their way to the Meet, calling to each other in high-pitched voices it was fun to imitate.

Later in the day they would often be seen galloping full-stretch over the fields and then the men at work there would drop their tools and climb on the five-barred gates for a better view, or stop their teams and straighten their backs at the plough-tail to cup their hands to their mouths and shout: 'Tally-ho: A-gallop, a-gallop, a-lye, a-lye, Tally-ho.'

When the carriages passed through, many of the women would set down the buckets they were carrying and curtsey, and the boys would pull their forelocks and the girls bob their knees, as they had been taught to do at school. This was an awkward moment for Laura, because her father had said, while he had no objection to Edmund saluting any lady – though he hoped, for heaven's sake, he would not do it by pulling his own hair, like pulling a bell-rope – he was determined that no daughter of his should bow the knee, excepting at 'The Name' in church or to Queen Victoria, if ever she happened to pass that way. Their mother laughed. 'When at Rome do as the Romans do,' she said.

'This is not Rome,' their father retorted. 'It's Lark Rise – the spot God made with the left-overs when He'd finished creating the rest of the earth.'

At that their mother tossed her head and clicked her tongue against the roof of her mouth. She had, as she said, no patience with some of his ideas.

Apart from the occasional carriages and the carrier's cart twice a week, there was little traffic on that road beyond the baker's van and the farm carts and wagons. Sometimes a woman from a neighbouring village or hamlet would pass through on foot, shopping basket on arm, on her way to the market town. It was thought nothing of then to walk six or seven miles to purchase a reel of cotton or a packet of tea, or sixpen'orth of pieces from the butcher to make a meat pudding for Sunday. Excepting the carrier's cart, which only came on certain days, there was no other way of travelling. It was thought quite dashing to ride with Old Jimmy, but frightfully extravagant, for the fare was sixpence. Most people preferred to go on foot and keep the sixpence to spend when they got there.

But, although it was not yet realized, the revolution in transport had begun. The first high 'penny-farthing' bicycles were already on the roads, darting and swerving like swallows heralding the summer of the buses and cars and motor cycles which were soon to transform country life. But how fast those new bicycles travelled and how dangerous they looked! Pedestrians backed almost into the hedges when they met one of them, for was there not almost every week in the Sunday newspaper the story of some one being knocked down and killed by a bicycle, and letters from readers saying cyclists ought not to be allowed to use the roads, which, as everybody knew, were provided for people to walk on or to drive on behind horses. 'Bicyclists ought to have roads to themselves, like railway trains' was the general opinion.

Yet it was thrilling to see a man hurtling through space on one high wheel, with another tiny wheel wobbling helplessly behind. You wondered how they managed to keep their balance. No wonder they wore an anxious air. 'Bicyclist's face', the expression was called, and the newspapers foretold a hunch-backed and tortured-faced future generation as a result of the pastime.

Cycling was looked upon as a passing craze and the cyclists in their tight navy knickerbocker suits and pillbox caps with the badge of their club in front were regarded as figures of fun. None of those in the hamlet who rushed out to their gates to see one pass, half hoping for and half fearing a spill, would have believed, if they had been told, that in a few years there would be at least one bicycle in every one of their houses, that the men would ride to work on them and the younger women, when their housework was done, would lightly mount 'the old bike' and pedal away to the market town to see the shops. They would have been still more incredulous had they been told that many of them would live to see every child of school age in the hamlet provided by a kind County Council with a bicycle on which they would ride to school, 'all free, gratis, and for nothing', as they would have said.

In the outer world men were running up tall factory chimneys and covering the green fields for miles with rows of mean little houses to house the workers. Towns which were already towns were throwing out roads and roads of suburban villas. New churches and chapels and railway stations and schools and public houses were being built to meet the needs of a fast-growing population. But the hamlet people saw none of these changes. They were far from the industrial districts and their surroundings remained as they had been from the time of their birth. No cottage had been added to the little group in the fields for many years, and, as it turned out, none were to be added for at least a half century; perhaps never, for the hamlet stands today unchanged in its outward appearance.

Queen Victoria was on the throne. She had been well established there before either of Laura's parents were born, and it seemed to her and her brother that she had always been Queen and always would be. But plenty of elderly people could remember her Coronation and could tell them what church bells had pealed all day in the different villages and what oxen had been roasted whole and what bonfires had been lighted at night.

'Our little English rose', the Rector said had then been her subjects' name for her, and Laura often thought of that when she studied the portrait which hung, framed and glazed, in the place of honour in many of the cottages. It was that of a stout, middle-aged, rather cross-looking lady with a bright blue Garter ribbon across her breast and a crown on her head so tiny that it made her face look large.

'How does she keep it on?' asked Laura, for it looked as if the slightest movement would send it toppling.

'Don't you worry about that,' said her mother comfortably, 'she'll manage to keep that on for a good many more years, you'll see'; and she did, for another twenty.

To the country at large, the Queen was no longer 'Our little English rose'. She had become 'The Queen-Empress' or 'Victoria the Good, the mother of her people'. To the hamlet she was 'th' old Queen', or, sometimes 'th' poor old Queen', for was she not a widow? And it was said she was having none too easy a time with that son of hers, either. But they all agreed she was a good Queen, and when asked why, would reply, 'Because she's brought the price of the quartern loaf down' or 'Well, we have got peace under her, haven't we?'

Peace? Of course there was peace. War was something you read about in books, something rather exciting, if only the poor soldiers had not had to be killed, but all long ago and far away, something that could not possibly happen in our time.

But there had been a war not so very long ago, their father told them. He himself had been born on the day of the Battle of Alma. We had been fighting the Russians then, a hard and cruel lot who had thought might was right, but had found themselves mistaken. They couldn't make slaves of a free people.

Then there was the old man who came round every few months playing a penny whistle and begging. He was known as 'One-eyed Peg-leg' because he had lost an eye and part of a leg fighting before Sebastopol. His trouser leg was cut short at the knee, which was supported by what was then called a 'wooden leg', although it did not resemble a human leg very closely, being but a plain wooden stump, tapering slightly at the bottom, where it was finished off by a ferrule. 'Dot and carry one', they called the sound he made when walking.

Laura once heard old Peg-leg telling a neighbour about the loss of his living member. After a hit with a cannon-ball he had lain for twenty-four hours unattended on the battlefield. Then a surgeon had come and, without more ado, had sawn off the shattered portion. 'And didn't I just holler,' he said; ''specially when he dipped the stump into a bucket of boiling tar. That was afore th' nusses come.'

Before the nurses came. Laura knew what that meant, for there was a picture of Florence Nightingale in a book she had and her mother had read to her about 'the Lady with the Lamp', whose shadow was kissed by the wounded.

But these rumours of the war in the Crimea did not seem to the children to bring it any nearer to their own lifetime, and when, later, they read in their old-fashioned story books of families of good children helping their mothers to knit and roll bandages for the soldiers in Russia, it still seemed as unreal as any fairy tale.

The soldiers who had their homes in the hamlet were not looked upon as fighting men, but as young adventurers who had enlisted as the only way of seeing the world before they settled down to marriage and the plough-tail. Judging from their letters, often read aloud to groups at cottage doors, the only enemies they had to face were sand-storms, mosquitoes, heat stroke, or ague.

The children's Uncle Edmund's trials were of a different nature, because he was in Nova Scotia, where noses got frozen. But he, of course, was in the Royal Engineers, as all the soldiers on their father's side of the family were, for had they not got a trade in their hands? The family was a bit snobbish about this. In those simple days a man whose parents had apprenticed him to a trade was looked upon as established for life. 'Put a trade in his hands and he'll always be sure of a good living,' people would say of a promising boy. They had yet to learn the full meaning of such words as 'depression' and 'unemployment'. So it was always the *Royal* Engineers, even with the mother at the end house. Her own family favoured the Field Artillery, which, to be sure, was Royal, too, although this was not insisted upon.

Both Engineers and Artillery looked down a little on the county regiment, and that, in its turn, looked down on the Militia. No doubt the Militia men had their standards, too; probably they looked down upon the unenterprising youths left at home, 'chaps as hadn't the sprawl to go a-soldiering'. Those who timidly ventured to join the Militia seldom remained in it long. Almost always, before their first season's training was over, they wrote to their parents to say that they found soldiering such a fine life they had decided to transfer to 'the Regulars'. Then they came home on furlough in their scarlet tunics and pill-box caps and strolled around the hamlet twirling their canes and caressing their new moustaches before disappearing overseas to India or Egypt. For those left at home there was little excitement. Christmas, the Harvest Home and the Village Feast were the only holidays. No cinemas, no wireless, no excursions or motor coaches or dances in village halls in those days! A few of the youths and younger men played cricket in the summer. One young man was considered a good bowler locally and he would sometimes get up a team to play one of the neighbouring villages. This once led to a curious little conversation on his doorstep. A lady had alighted from her carriage to ask or, rather, command him to get up a team to play 'the young gentlemen', meaning her sons, on holidays from school, and a few of their friends. Naturally, Frank wanted to know the strength of the team he was to be up against. 'You'd want me to bring a good team, I suppose, ma'am?' he asked respectfully.

'Well, yes,' said the lady. 'The young gentlemen would enjoy a good game. But don't bring *too* good a team. They wouldn't want to be beaten.'

'That's what she calls cricket,' said Frank, grinning broadly at her retreating figure.

This country scene is only a little over fifty years distant from us in time; but in manners, customs and conditions of life, it is centuries away. Except that slates were superseding thatch for roofing and the old open hearth was giving place to the built-in grate, the cottages were as the dwellings of the poor had been for generations. The people still ate the old country fare, preferring it, so far, to such of the new factory-made products as had come their way. The smock frock was still worn by the older men, who declared that one well-made smock would outlast twenty of the new machine-made suits the younger men were buying. The smock, with its elaborately stitched yoke and snow-white home laundering, was certainly more artistic than the coarse, badly-fitting 'reach-me-downs', as they were sometimes called.

The women were more fashion-minded than the men, but their efforts to keep up-to-date were confined to the 'Sunday best' which they seldom took from their boxes upstairs. For everyday wear, they contented themselves with a large, well-ironed white apron to cover their patches and darns. To go to the well, or from house to house in the hamlet, they threw a plaid woollen shawl over their shoulders, or, in bad weather, drew it up to cover their heads. Then, with a strong pair of patterns under their feet, they were ready for anything.

They were still much as their forefathers had been; but change was creeping in, if slowly. A weekly newspaper came into every house, either by purchase or borrowing, and although these were still written by educated men for the educated and our hamlet intellects had sometimes to reach up a little for their ideas, ideas were slowly percolating.

Having to reach up for ideas came naturally to a generation brought up on the Bible. Their fathers had looked upon 'the Word' as their one unfailing guide in life's difficulties. It was their story book, their treasury of words and sayings, and, for those who could appreciate it, their one book of poetry. Many of the older people still believed every word in the Bible to be literally true. Others were not so sure; that tale of Jonah and the whale, for instance, took a good deal of swallowing. But the newspaper everybody believed in. 'I seed it in the paper, so it must be true' was a saying calculated to clinch any argument.

II

A Hamlet Home

Laura arrived on this scene on a cold December morning when snow lay in deep drifts over the fields and blocked the roads. There were no fireplaces in cottage bedrooms such as her mother's was, and the relays of hot bricks, baked in the oven and swathed in flannel, lost their warmth coming upstairs. 'Oh, we were so cold, so cold,' her mother would say when telling the story, and Laura liked that 'we'. It showed that even a tiny baby who had never been outside the room in which she was born was already a person.

Her parents' life was not quite so hard as that of most of their neighbours, for her father was a stonemason and earned more money than the farm-workers, although in the eighteen-eighties a skilled craftsman, such as he was, received little more in wages than today's unemployment pay.

He was not a native of those parts, but had been brought there a few years earlier by a firm of builders engaged in the restoration of some of the churches of the countryside. He was an expert workman and loved his craft. It was said that he would copy some crumbling detail of carving and fit it in in such a way that the original carver could not have detected the substitution. He did carving at home, too, in the little workshop he had built at the side of their cottage. A few of his attempts stood about as ornaments in the house, a lion, lilies of the valley growing at the base of a tree trunk, and a baby's head, perhaps Edmund's or Laura's. Whether these were well done or not Laura never knew, for before she was old enough to discriminate they had become grimy and been swept off to the rubbish heap; but it pleased her to know that he had at least the impulse to create and the skill to execute, however imperfectly.

By the time the restoration work was finished he had married and had two children and, though he never cared for the hamlet or became one with the little community there, as his wife and children did, he stayed behind when his workmates left and settled down to work as an ordinary stonemason.

There was still a good deal of building in stone going on in that part of the country. One country house had been burnt down and had to be rebuilt; another had a new wing added, and, afterwards, he would make a tombstone, build a cottage or wall, set a grate, or lay a few bricks as required. Workmen were expected to turn their hands to anything within the limits of their trade, and he who could do most was considered the better workman. The day of the specialist was in the future. Each workman must keep to his trade, however. Laura remembered that once, when frost prevented him from working, he happened to say to her mother that the carpenters had plenty to do, and when her mother, knowing that he had been through all the shops, as was the custom with builders' sons at that time, asked why he could not ask to be allowed to do some carpentering, he laughed and said: 'The carpenters would have something to say about that! They would say I was poaching, and tell me to keep to my own trade.'

For thirty-five years he was employed by a firm of builders in the market town, walking the three miles, night and morning, at first; cycling later. His hours were from six in the morning to five in the afternoon, and to reach his work in time he had for the greater part of the year to leave home before daylight.

As Laura first remembered him he was a slim, upright young man in the late twenties, with dark, fiery eyes and raven-black hair, but fair, fresh-coloured complexion. On account of the dusty-white nature of his work, he usually wore clothes of some strong light-grey worsted material. Years after he had died, an old and embittered man, she could see him, a white apron rolled up around his middle, a basket of tools slung over his shoulder and a black billycock hat set at an angle on his head, swinging along on the crown of the road on his way home from work, looking, as the hamlet people said, 'as if he had bought all the land on one side of the road and was thinking of buying that on the other side'.

Even in darkness his step could be distinguished, for it was lighter and sharper than that of the other men. His mind moved more quickly, too, and his tongue was readier, for he belonged to another breed and had been brought up in another environment.

Some of the neighbours thought him proud and 'set up with himself ', but he was tolerated for his wife's sake and his relations with the neighbours were at least outwardly friendly – especially at Election time, when he mounted a plank supported by two beer-barrels and expounded the Gladstonian programme, while Laura, her eyes on a level with his best buttoned boots, quaked inwardly lest he should be laughed at.

His audience of twenty or so laughed quite a lot, but with him, not at him, for he was an amusing speaker. None of them knew and probably he himself had not begun to suspect that they were listening to a lost and thwarted man, one who had strayed into a life to which he did not belong and one whose own weakness would keep him there for the rest of his days.

Already he was beginning to keep irregular hours. Their mother, telling them a bedtime story, would glance up at the clock and say: 'Wherever has Daddy got to?' or, later in the evening, more severely, 'Your father's staying late again', and when he came in his face would be flushed and he would be more than usually talkative. But that was only the beginning of his downfall. Things went well, or fairly well, for several years after that.

Their cottage belonged to a Mrs Herring. She and her husband had lived there for some time before Laura's parents had rented it, but, as he was an ex-stud groom with a pension and she prided herself on her superiority, they had never been happy or popular there. Her superiority might have been borne, or even played up to, for 'you've got to hold a candle to the fire', as some of the neighbours said, but it was accompanied by the to them intolerable vice of meanness. Not only had she kept herself to herself, as she boasted, but she had also kept her belongings to herself, down to the last shred of 'scratchings' when she boiled down her lard and the last cabbage-stalk from the garden. 'She wer' that near she 'udn't give away enough to make a pair of leggings for a skylark' was the reputation she left behind her.

She, on her side, had complained that the hamlet people were a rough, unmannerly lot. There was nobody fit to ask in for a game of cards and she did so like a bit of society, and she had long wanted to go to live near her married daughter, when, one Saturday afternoon, the children's father came, looking for a cottage not too far from his work. She made a great favour of getting out quickly, but her new tenants were not impressed, for she was asking a high rent, half a crown a week, more than anyone else in the hamlet paid. The neighbours had thought she would never let her house, for who could afford to pay that sum?

Laura's parents, with more knowledge of town prices, thought the house was well worth the rent, for it was two small thatched cottages made into one, with two bedrooms and a good garden. Of course, as they said, it had not the conveniences of a town house. Until they themselves had bought an oven grate and put it in the second cottage downstairs room, known as 'the wash-house', there was nowhere to bake the Sunday joint, and it was tiresome to have to draw water up from a well and irritating in wet weather to have to walk under an umbrella half-way down the garden to the earth closet. But the cottage living-room was a pleasant place, with its well-polished furniture, shelves of bright crockery, and red-and-black rugs laid down to 'take the tread' on the raddled tile floor.

In summer the window stood permanently open and hollyhocks and other tall flowers would push their way in and mingle with the geraniums and fuchsias on the window-sill.

This room was the children's nursery. Their mother called it that sometimes when they had been cutting out pictures and left scraps of paper on the floor. 'This room's nothing but a nursery,' she would say, forgetting for the moment that the nurseries she had presided over in her pre-marriage days were usually held up by her as patterns of neatness.

The room had one advantage over most nurseries. The door

opened straight out on to the garden path and in fine weather the children were allowed to run in and out as they would. Even when it rained and a board was slipped, country fashion, into grooves in the doorposts to keep them in, they could still lean out over it and feel the rain splash on their hands and see the birds flicking their wings in the puddles and smell the flowers and wet earth while they sang: 'Rain, rain, go away, Come again another day.'

They had more garden than they needed at that time and one corner was given up to a tangle of currant and gooseberry bushes and raspberry canes surrounding an old apple tree. This jungle, as their father called it, was only a few feet square, but a child of five or seven could hide there and pretend it was lost, or hollow out a cave in the greenery and call it its house. Their father kept saying that he must get busy and lop the old unproductive apple tree and cut down the bushes to let in the light and air, but he was so seldom at home in daylight that for a long time nothing was done about it and they still had their hidy-houses and could still swing themselves up and ride astride on the low-hanging limb of the apple tree.

From there they could see the house and their mother going in and out, banging mats and rattling pails and whitening the flagstones around the doorway. Sometimes, when she went to the well, they would run after her and she would hold them tight and let them look down to where, framed in the green-slimy stones, the water reflected their faces, very small and far down.

'You must never come here alone,' she would say. 'I once knew a little boy who was drowned in a well like this.' Then, of course, they wanted to know where and when and why he was drowned, although they had heard the story as long as they could remember. 'Where was his mother?' 'Why was the well lid left open?' 'How did they get him out?' and 'Was he quite, quite dead? As dead as the mole we saw under the hedge one day?'

Beyond their garden in summer were fields of wheat and barley and oats which sighed and rustled and filled the air with sleepy pollen and earth scents. These fields were large and flat and stretched away to a distant line of trees set in the hedgerows. To the children at that time these trees marked the boundary of their world. Tall trees and smaller trees and one big bushy squat tree like a crouching animal – they knew the outline of each one by heart and looked upon them as children in more hilly districts look upon the peaks of distant, unvisited, but familiar mountains.

Beyond their world, enclosed by the trees, there was, they were told, a wider world, with other hamlets and villages and towns and the sea, and, beyond that, other countries where the people spoke languages different from their own. Their father had told them so. But, until they learned to read, they had no mental picture of these, they were but ideas, unrealized; whereas, in their own little world within the tree boundary, everything appeared to them more than life-size and more richly coloured.

They knew every slight rise in the fields and the moist lower places where the young wheat grew taller and greener, and the bank where the white violets grew, and the speciality of every hedgerow – honeysuckle, crab-apples, misty purple sloes, or long trails of white bryony berries through which the sun shone crimson as it did through the window at church: *'But you must not even touch one or your hand will poison your food.'*

And they knew the sounds of the different seasons, the skylarks singing high up out of sight over the green corn; the loud, metallic chirring of the mechanical reaper, the cheerful 'Who-o-as' and 'Werts up' of the ploughmen to their teams, and the rush of wings as the starlings wheeled in flocks over the stripped stubble.

There were other shadows than those of chasing clouds and wheeling bird flocks over those fields. Ghost stories and stories of witchcraft lingered and were half believed. No one cared to go after dark to the crossroads where Dickie Bracknell, the suicide, was buried with a stake through his entrails, or to approach the barn out in the fields where he had hung himself some time at the beginning of the century. Bobbing lights were said to have been seen and gurgling sounds heard there.

Far out in the fields by the side of a wood was a pool which was said to be bottomless and haunted by a monster. No one could say exactly what the monster was like, for no one living had seen it, but the general idea was that it resembled a large newt, perhaps as big as a bullock. Among the children this pool was known as 'the beast's pond' and none of them ever went near it. Few people went that way, for the pond was cut off from the fields by a piece of unculti-vated waste, and there was no path anywhere near it. Some fathers and mothers did not believe there was a pond there. It was just a silly old tale, they said, that folks used at one time to frighten themselves with. But there was a pond, for, towards the end of their schooldays, Edmund and Laura plodded over several ploughed fields and scrambled through as many hedges and pushed their way through a waste of dried thistles and ragwort and stood at last by a dark, still, tree-shadowed pool. No monster was there, only dark water, dark trees and a darkening sky and a silence so deep they could hear their own hearts pounding.

Nearer home, beside the brook, was an old elder tree which was said to bleed human blood when cut, and that was because it was no ordinary tree, but a witch. Men and boys of a former generation had caught her listening outside the window of a neighbour's cottage and chased her with pitchforks until she reached the brook. Then, being a witch, she could not cross running water, so had turned herself into an elder tree on the bank.

She must have turned herself back again, for, the next morning, she was seen fetching water from the well as usual, a poor, ugly, disagreeable old woman who denied having been outside her own door the night before. But the tree, which hitherto no one had noticed, still stood beside the brook and was still standing there fifty years later. Edmund and Laura once took a table knife, intending to cut it, but their courage failed them. 'What if it should really bleed? And what if the witch came out of it and ran after us?'

'Mother,' asked Laura one day, 'are there any witches now?' and her mother answered seriously, 'No. They seem to have all died out. There haven't been any in my time; but when I was your age there were plenty of old people alive who had known or even been ill-wished by one. And, of course,' she added as an afterthought, 'we know there were witches. We read about them in the Bible.' That settled it. Anything the Bible said must be true.

Edmund was at that time a quiet, thoughtful little boy, apt to ask questions which it puzzled his mother to answer. The neighbours said he thought too much and ought to be made to play more; but they liked him because of his good looks and quaint, old-fashioned good manners. Except when he fired questions at them.

'I shan't tell you,' some one would say when cornered by him. 'If I told you that you'd know as much as I do myself. Besides, what do it matter to you what makes the thunder and lightning. You sees it and hears it and are lucky if you're not struck dead by it, and that ought to be enough for you.' Others, more kindly disposed, or more talkative, would tell him that the thunder was the voice of God. Somebody had been wicked, perhaps Edmund himself, and God was angry; or that thunder was caused by the clouds knocking together; or warn him to keep away from trees during a thunder-storm because they had known a man who was struck dead while sheltering and the watch in his pocket had melted and run like quicksilver down his legs. Others would quote:

> Under oak there comes a stroke,
> Under elm there comes a calm,
> And under ash there comes a crash,

and Edmund would retire into himself to sort out this information.

He was a tall, slender child with blue eyes and regular features. When she had dressed him for their afternoon walk, his mother would kiss him and exclaim: 'I do declare he might be anybody's child. I can't see any difference between him and a young lord, and as for intelligence, he's too intelligent!'

Setting out on these walks, Laura must have looked a prim, old-fashioned little thing in her stiffly starched frock, with a white silk scarf tied in a bow under her chin and a couple of inches of knicker frill showing. 'Odd', the neighbours called her when dis-cussing her in her presence, for she had dark eyes and pale yellow hair, and they did not approve of the mixture. 'Pity she ain't got your eyes,' they would say to her mother whose own eyes were blue; 'or even if she had dark hair like her father, 'twouldn't be so bad, but, as 'tis, she ain't neither one thing nor t'other. Cross-grained,

they say them folks is whose eyes and hair don't match. But' –
turning to Laura – 'never you mind, my poppet. Good looks ain't
everything, and you can't help it if you did happen to be behind the
door when they were being given out. And, after all' – comfortingly
to her mother – 'she don't hurt, really. She's got a nice bit of colour
in her cheeks.'

'You're all right. Always keep yourself clean and neat and try to
have a pleasant, good-tempered expression, and you'll pass in a
crowd,' her mother told her.

But that did not satisfy Laura. She was bent on improvement.
She could not alter her eyes, but she tried to darken her hair with
ink, put on in streaks with her father's new toothbrush. That only
resulted in a sore bottom and lying in bed by daylight with her
newly washed hair in tiny tight plaits which hurt her head. However,
to her great joy, her hair soon began to darken naturally, and, after
many false alarms, one of which was the fear it was turning red, it
became a respectable brown, quite unnoticeable.

Other memories of those early years remained with her as little
pictures, without background, and unrelated to anything which
went before or came after. One was of walking over frosty fields
with her father, her small knitted-gloved hand reaching up to his
big knitted-gloved hand and the stubble beneath their feet clinking
with little icicles until they came to a pinewood and crept under a
rail and walked on deep, soft earth beneath tall, dark trees.

The wood was so dark and silent at first that it was almost
frightening; but, soon, they heard the sounds of axes and saws at
work and came out into a clearing where men were felling trees.
They had built themselves a little house of pine branches and before
it a fire was burning. The air was full of the sharp, piny scent of the
smoke which drifted across the clearing in blue whorls and lay in
sheets about the boughs of the unfelled trees beyond. Laura and her
father sat on a tree-trunk before the fire and drank hot tea, which
was poured for them from a tin can. Then her father filled the sack
he had brought with logs and Laura's little basket was piled with
shiny brown pine-cones and they went home. They must have gone
home, although no trace of memory remained of the backward

journey: only the joy of drinking hot tea so far from a house and the loveliness of shooting flames and blue smoke against blue-green pine boughs survived.

Another memory was of a big girl, with red hair, in a bright blue frock billowing over a green field, looking for mushrooms, and a man at the gate taking his clay pipe from his mouth to whisper behind his hand to a companion: 'That gal'll tumble to bits before they get her to church if they don't look sharp.'

'Patty tumble to bits? Tumble to bits? How could she?' Laura's mother looked rather taken aback when asked, and told her little daughter she must never, never listen to men talking. It was naughty to do that. Then she explained, rather lamely for her, that Patty must have done something wrong. Perhaps she'd told a lie, and Mr Arliss was afraid she might be struck dead, like the man and woman in the Bible. 'You remember them? I told you about them when you said you saw a ghost coming out of the clothes closet upstairs.'

That reference to her own misdeed sent Laura out to creep under the gooseberry bushes in the garden, where she thought it would puzzle even God to find her; but she was not satisfied. Why should Mr Arliss mind if Patty had told a lie? Plenty of people told them and no one, so far, had been struck dead at Lark Rise.

Forty years after, her mother laughed when reminded of this. 'Poor old Pat!' she said. 'She was a regular harum-scarum and no mistake. But they did just manage to get her to church, although it was said at the time they had to give her a sup of brandy in the porch. Howsoever, she recovered enough to dance at the wedding, I heard, and a fine sight she must have looked in a white frock with blue bows all down the front. I think that was the last time I ever heard of taking round the hat to collect for the cradle at a wedding. It used to be quite the usual thing with that class of people at one time.'

Then there was the picture of a man lying on straw at the bottom of a farm cart with a white cloth over his face. The cart had halted outside one of the houses and apparently the news of its arrival had not got round, for, at first, only Laura was standing by. The tailboard of the cart had been removed and she could see the man plainly, lying so still, so terribly still, that she thought he was dead. It seemed a long time to her before his wife rushed out, climbed into the car, and calling, 'My dear one! My poor old man!' took the cloth from his face, revealing a face almost as white, excepting for one long dark gash from lips to one ear. Then he groaned and Laura's heart began beating again.

The neighbours gathered round and the story spread. He was a stockman and had been feeding his fattening beasts when one of them had accidentally caught a horn in his mouth and torn his cheek open. He was taken at once to the Cottage Hospital in the market town and his wound soon healed.

An especially vivid memory was of an April evening when Laura was about three. Her mother had told her that the next day was May Day and that Alice Shaw was going to be May Queen and wear a daisy crown. 'I should like to be May Queen and wear a daisy crown. Can't I have one, too, Mother?' asked Laura.

'So you shall,' her mother replied. 'You run down to the play place and pick some daisies and I'll make you a crown. You shall be our May Queen.'

Off she ran with her little basket, but by the time she reached the plot of rough grass where the hamlet children played their country games it was too late; the sun had set, and the daisies were all asleep. There were thousands and thousands of them, but all screwed up, like tightly shut eyes. Laura was so disappointed that she sat down in the midst of them and cried. Only a few tears and very soon dried, then she began to look about her. The long grass in which she sat was a little wet, perhaps with dew, or perhaps from an April shower, and the pink-tipped daisy buds were a little wet, too, like eyes that had gone to sleep crying. The sky, where the sun had set, was all pink and purple and primrose. There was no one in sight and no sound but the birds singing and, suddenly, Laura realized that it was nice to be there, out of doors by herself, deep in the long grass, with the birds and the sleeping daisies.

A little later in her life came the evening after a pig-killing when she stood alone in the pantry where the dead animal hung suspended from a hook in the ceiling. Her mother was only a few feet away. She could hear her talking cheerfully to Mary Ann, the girl who fetched their milk from the farm and took the children for walks when their mother was busy. Through the thin wooden partition she could hear her distinctive giggle as she poured water from a jug into the long, slippery lengths of chitterlings her mother was manipulating. Out there in the wash-house they were busy and cheerful, but in the pantry where Laura stood was a dead, cold silence.

She had known that pig all its life. Her father had often held her over the door of its sty to scratch its back and she had pushed lettuce and cabbage stalks through the bars for it to enjoy. Only that morning it had routed and grunted and squealed because it had had no breakfast. Her mother had said its noise got on her nerves and her father had looked uncomfortable, although he had passed it off by saying: 'No. No breakfast today, piggy. You're going to have a big operation by and by and there's no breakfast before operations.'

Now it had had its operation and there it hung, cold and stiff and so very, very dead. Not funny at all any more, but in some queer way dignified. The butcher had draped a long, lacy piece of fat from its own interior over one of its forelegs, in the manner in which ladies of that day sometimes carried a white lacy shawl, and that last touch seemed to Laura utterly heartless. She stayed there a long time, patting its hard, cold side and wondering that a thing so recently full of life and noise could be so still. Then, hearing her mother call her, she ran out of the door farthest from where she was working lest she should be scolded for crying over a dead pig.

There was fried liver and fat for supper and when Laura said, 'No, thank you,' her mother looked at her rather suspiciously, then said: 'Well, perhaps better not, just going to bed and all; but here's a nice bit of sweetbread. I was saving it for Daddy, but you have it. You'll like that.' And Laura ate the sweetbread and dipped her bread in the thick, rich gravy and refused to think about the poor pig in the pantry, for, although only five years old, she was learning to live in this world of compromises.

III

'Once Upon a Time'

No one who saw Laura's mother at that time would have wondered at the hasty, youthful marriage which turned her husband's contemplated sojourn of a few months into a permanent abode. She was a slight, graceful girl with a wild-rose complexion and hair the colour of a new penny which she parted in the middle and drew down to a knot at the back of her head because a gentleman of the family, where she had been nurse to the children before her marriage, had told her she ought always to do it like that.

'A pocket Venus,' she said he had called her. 'But quite nicely,' she hastened to assure her listener, 'for he was a married gentleman with no nonsense about him.' Another thing she told her children about her nursing days was that when visitors were staying in the house it was the custom for some member of the family to bring them up to the nursery after dinner to listen to the bed-time stories she was telling the children. 'A regular amusement,' she said it was with them, and her own children did not think that at all strange, for the bed-time stories were now being told to them and they knew how exciting they were.

Some of them were short stories, begun and finished in an evening, fairy stories and animal stories and stories of good and bad children, the good ones rewarded and the bad ones punished, according to the convention of that day. A few of these were part of the stock-in-trade of all tellers of stories to children, but far more of them were of her own invention, for she said it was easier to make up a tale than to try to remember one. The children liked her own stories best. 'Something out of your own head, Mother,' they would beg, and she would wrinkle up her brow and pretend to think hard, then begin: 'Once upon a time.'

One story remained with Laura long after hundreds of others had become a blur of pleasurable memory. Not because it was one of her mother's best, for it was not, but because it had a colour scheme which appealed to a childish taste. It was about a little girl who crept under a bush on a heath, 'just like Hardwick Heath, where we went blackberrying, you know', and found a concealed opening which led to an underground palace in which all the furniture and hangings were pale blue and silver. 'Silver tables and silver chairs and silver plates to eat off and all the cushions and curtains made of pale blue satin.' The heroine had marvellous adventures, but they left no impression on Laura's mind, while the blue and silver, deep down under the earth, shone with a kind of moonlight radiance in her imagination. But when her mother, at her urgent request, tried to tell the story again the magic was gone, although she introduced silver floors and silver ceilings, hoping to please her. Perhaps she overdid it.

Then there were serial stories which went on in nightly instalments for weeks, or perhaps months, for nobody wanted them to end and the teller's invention never flagged. There was one, however, which came to a sudden and tragic conclusion. One night when it was bedtime, or past bedtime, and the children had begged for more and been given it and were still begging for more, their mother lost patience and startled them both by saying, 'and then he came to the sea and fell in and was eaten by a shark, and that was the end of poor Jimmy', and the end of their story, too, for what further developments were possible?

Then there were the family stories, each one of which they knew by heart and could just as well have told to each other. Their favourite was the one they called 'Granny's Golden Footstool'. It was short and simple enough. Their father's parents had at one time kept a public-house and livery stables in Oxford and the story ran that, either going to, or coming from, the 'Horse and Rider', their grandfather had handed their grandmother into the carriage and placed a box containing a thousand pounds in gold at her feet, saying: 'It's not every lady who can ride in her own carriage with a golden footstool.'

They must have been on their way there with the purchase money, for they can have brought no golden footstool away with them. Before that adventure, made possible by a legacy left to the grandmother by one of her relatives, the grandfather had been a builder in a small way, and, after it, he went back to building again, in a still smaller way, presumably, for by the time Laura was born the family business had disappeared and her father was working for wages.

The thousand pounds had vanished as completely as Jimmy after the shark had eaten him, and all they could do about it was to try to imagine what so much gold together must have looked like and to plan what they would do with such a sum if they had it now. Even their mother liked talking about it, although, as she said, she had no patience with wasteful, extravagant ways, such as some people she knew had got, and them proud and set up when they ought to be ashamed of themselves for coming down in the world.

And, just as they prided themselves on the golden footstool and the accompanying tradition that their grandmother was 'a lady by birth' who had made a runaway marriage with their grandfather, almost every family in the hamlet prided itself upon some family tradition which, in its own estimation, at least, raised it above the common mass of the wholly uninteresting. An uncle or a great-uncle had owned a cottage which, in the course of time, had been magnified into a whole row of houses; or some one in the family had once kept a shop or a public-house, or farmed his own land. Or they boasted of good blood, even if it came illegitimately. One man claimed to be the great-grandson of an earl, 'on the wrong side of the blanket, of course,' he admitted; but he liked to talk about it, and his listener, noticing, perhaps for the first time, his fine figure and big, hooked nose, and considering the reputation of a certain wild young nobleman of a former generation, would feel inclined to believe there was some foundation for his story.

Another of Edmund and Laura's family stories, more fantastic, though not so well substantiated as that of the golden footstool, was that one of their mother's uncles, when a very young man, shut his father in a box and himself ran away to the Australian goldfields. In answer to their questions as to why he had shut his father up in a box, how he had got him into it, and how the father had got out again, their mother could only say that she did not know. It had all happened before her own father was born. It was a large family and he was the youngest. But she had seen the box: it was a long oak coffer that could well have held a man, and that was the story she had been told as long as she could remember.

That must have been eighty years before, and the uncle was never heard of again, but they never tired of talking about him and wondering if he found any gold. Perhaps he had made a fortune at the diggings and died without children and without making a will. Then the money would be theirs, wouldn't it? Perhaps it was even now in Chancery, waiting for them to claim it. Several families in the hamlet had money in Chancery. They knew it was there because one of the Sunday newspapers printed each week a list of names of people who had fortunes waiting, and their names had been there, in print, 'as large as life and twice as natural'. True, as the children's father said, most of their names were common ones, but if this was pointed out to them they were quite offended and hinted that when they could raise a few pounds to 'hire a lawyer chap' to set about claiming it, no disbeliever would participate.

The children had not seen their names in print, but they enjoyed planning what they would do with their Chancery money. Edmund said he would buy a ship and visit every country in the world. Laura thought she would like a house full of books in the middle of a wood, and their mother declared she would be quite satisfied if she had an income of thirty shillings a week, 'paid regular and to be depended upon'.

Their Chancery money was a chimera, and none of them through-out their lives had more than a few pounds at a time, but their wishes were more or less granted. Edmund crossed the sea many times and saw four out of the five continents; Laura had her house full of books, if not actually in a wood, with a wood somewhere handy; and their poor mother, towards the end of her life, got her modest thirty shillings a week, for that was the exact sum to which the Canadian Government made up her small income when granting her her Mother's Pension. The memory of that wish gave an added bitterness to the tears she shed for the first few years when the monthly cheque arrived.

But all that was far in the future on those winter evenings when they sat in the firelight, the two children on little stools at their mother's feet, while she knitted their socks and told them stories or sang. They had had their evening meal and their father's plate stood over a saucepan of water on the hob, keeping warm. Laura loved to watch the warm light flickering on the walls, lighting up one thing after another and casting dark shadows, including their own, more than life-size and excitingly grotesque.

Edmund joined in the chorus of such things as 'There is a Tavern' and 'Little Brown Jug' but Laura refrained, by special request, for she had no ear for music and they said her singing put them out of tune. But she loved to watch the firelight shadows and to hear her mother's voice singing to sweet melancholy airs of a pale host of fair maidens who pined and faded for love. There was 'Lily Lyle, Sweet Lily Lyle', which began:

> 'Twas a still, calm night and the moon's pale light
>> Shone over hill and dale
> When friends mute with grief stood around the deathbed
>> Of their loved, lost Lily Lyle.
>> Heart as pure as forest lily,
>>> Never knowing guile,
>> Had its home within the bosom
>>> Of sweet Lily Lyle.

Several other dying maidens were celebrated in similar words to similar airs. Then there was 'The Old Armchair' and 'The Gipsy's Warning' and a group of cottage songs apparently dating from the beginning of the century, such as:

'Twas a fine clear night and the moon shone bright
  When the village clock struck eight
And Mary hastened with delight
  Unto the garden gate.

But what was there that made her sad?
The gate was there, but not the lad,
  Which caused poor Mary to sigh and say,
'He never shall make a goose of me.'

She traced the garden here and there and the village clock struck
    nine,
  Which caused poor Mary to sigh and say,
'He never shall be mine.'

She traced the garden here and there and the village clock struck
    ten,
  Young William caught her in his arms,
Never to part again.

Now he'd been to buy the ring that day and he had been such a
    long, long way,
  So how could Mary so cruel prove
As to banish the lad whom she dearly loved?

So down in a cot by the riverside
William and Mary now reside.
And she's blessed the hour that she did wait
For her absent lover at the garden gate.

Sometimes the children would talk about what they would do
when they were grown up. Their fortune had already been mapped
out for them. Edmund was to be apprenticed to a trade – a carpenter's, their mother thought; it was cleaner work than that of a mason
and carpenters did not drink in public-houses as masons did, and
people respected them more.

Laura was to go as nursemaid under one of her mother's old nurse friends with whom she had kept up a correspondence. Then, in time, she would be head nurse herself in what was then known as 'a good family'; where, if she did not marry, she would be sure of a home for life, for the imaginary good family her mother had in mind was of the kind where loved old nurses dressed in black silk and had a room of their own in which to receive confidences. But these ideas did not interest the children so much as that of having houses of their own in which they could do as they liked. 'And you'll come to stay with me and I shall spring-clean the house and bake some pies the day before,' promised Laura, who knew from her mother's example what was due to an honoured guest. Edmund's idea was that he would have treacle mixed with milk for dinner without any bread at all, but then he was much younger than she was.

Neither story-telling, singing, nor talking could go on for ever. The time always came, and always came too soon for them, when their mother would whisk them off to bed, 'For your father cannot be much longer now,' and stay to hear them say their prayers, 'Our Father' and 'Gentle Jesus', then 'Gawbless dear Mammy an' Daddy an' dear little brother [or sister] an' all kind friends an' alations . . .'

Laura was not sure who the friends were, but she knew that the relations included the Candleford aunts, her father's sisters, who sent them nice parcels at Christmas, and the cousins whose wardrobes she inherited. The aunts were kind – she knew that, for when she opened the parcels her mother would say, 'It's very kind of Edith, I'm sure,' or, more warmly, although the parcel might not be as exciting, 'If ever there was a good kind soul in this world, it's your Aunt Ann.'

Candleford was a wonderful place. Her mother said there were rows of shops there, simply stuffed with toys and sweets and furs and muffs and watches and chains and other delightful things. 'You should see them at Christmas,' she said, 'all lit up like a fair. All you want then is a purseful of money!' The Candleford people had pursefuls of money, for wages were higher there, and they had gas to light them to bed and drew their water out of taps, instead of up from a well. She had heard her parents say so. 'What he wants is a job at some place such as Candleford,' her father would say of some promising boy. 'He'd do himself some good there. Here, there's nothing.' This surprised Laura, for she had thought there were many exciting things about the hamlet. 'Is there a brook there?' she asked, rather hoping there was not, and she was told there was a river, which was wider than any brook and had a stone bridge, instead of a rickety old plank to cross by. A magnificent place, indeed, and she hoped soon to see it. 'Come the summer' her father had said, but the summer had come and gone again and nothing more had been said about borrowing Polly and the spring cart. Then, always, something or other happened to push the idea of Candleford to the back of her mind. One dreary November the pigs were ill. They refused to eat and became so weak they had to lean against the rails of their sties for support. Some of them died and were buried in quicklime, which was said to burn up their bodies in no time. Horrible thought to be dead and buried in quicklime and soon nothing left of what had been so much alive! Her mother said it was a far worse thought that the poor people had lost their pigs, after paying for their food all those months, too, and when their own pigs were killed – both had escaped – she was more than usually generous with the plates of liver and fat and other oddments always sent to neighbours as a compliment. Many of the people who had lost their pigs still owed for the food. They had depended upon being able to pay for that in kind when the animal was fattened. One man took to poaching and was caught and sent to prison, then every one had to take half loaves and small screws of tea and sugar to help his wife to keep the home going, until the whisper went round that she had three different lots of butter in the house, given by different people to whom she had pleaded poverty, and that the J.P. himself had sent a sovereign. People looked sourly upon her after that was known, and said, 'Crime seems to pay nowadays.'

IV

'A Bit of a Tell'

Sometimes, instead of saying, 'Here there's nothing,' her father would say, 'Here there's nobody,' meaning nobody he thought worth considering. But Laura never tired of considering the hamlet neighbours, and, as she grew older, would listen to, and piece together, the things they said until she had learned quite a lot from them. She liked the older women best such as Old Queenie, Old Sally, and Old Mrs Prout, old countrywomen who still wore sunbonnets and stayed in their own homes and gardens and cared not at all about what was in fashion and very little for gossip. They said they did not hold with gadding about from house to house. Queenie had her lace-making and her beehives to watch; Old Sally her brewing and her bacon to cure; if anybody wanted to see them, they knew where to find them. 'Crusty old dames,' some of the younger women called them, especially when one of them had refused to lend them something. To Laura they seemed like rocks, keeping firm in their places, while those about them drifted around, always on the look-out for some new sensation. But only a few were left who kept to the old country ways, and the other women were interesting, too. Although they wore much the same kind of clothes and lived in similar houses, no two of them were really alike.

In theory all the hamlet women were on friendly terms with each other, at least as far as 'passing the time of day' when they met, for they had an almost morbid dread of giving offence and would go out of their way to be pleasant to other women they would rather not have seen. As Laura's mother said: 'You can't *afford* to be on bad terms with anybody in a small place like this.' But in that, as in more sophisticated societies, there was a tendency to form sets. The members of the slightly more prosperous of these, consisting mostly of the newly married and those of the older women whose children were grown up and off their hands, would change into a clean apron in the afternoon and stay quietly at home, sewing or ironing, or put on their hats and go out to call upon their friends, carefully knocking at the door before they lifted the latch. The commoner kind burst hatless into their neighbour's houses to borrow something or to relate some breathless item of news, or they would spend the afternoon shouting it across gardens or from doorsteps, or hold long, bantering conversations with the baker, or the oilman, or any one else who happened to call and found themselves unable to get away without downright rudeness.

Laura's mother belonged to the first category and those who came to her house were mostly her own special friends. They had a few other callers, however, and those Laura thought far more interesting than young Mrs Massey, who was always making baby's clothes, although at that time she had no baby (Laura thought afterwards, when a baby arrived for her, it was a lucky coincidence), or Mrs Hadley, who was always talking about her daughter in service, or Mrs Finch, who was 'not too strong' and had to be given the best seat, nearest the fire. The only interesting thing about her was the little blue bottle of smelling-salts she carried, and that ceased to interest after she had handed it to Laura, telling her to give a good sniff, then laughed when the tears ran down her cheeks. Not at all Laura's idea of a joke!

She liked Rachel much better. Although never invited, she would drift in sometimes, 'just to have a tell', as she expressed it. Her 'tells' were worth hearing, for she knew everything that happened, 'and a good lot more, too', her enemies said. 'Ask Rachel,' some one would say with a shrug if the whole of the facts of a happening were not known, and Rachel, when appealed to, if she, too, were not quite sure, would say in her loud, hearty voice, 'Well to tell the truth, I haven't ever quite got to the bottom of that business. But I 'ull know, that I 'ull, for I'll go to th' fountain-head and ax.' And off she would march with all the good-natured effrontery imaginable to ask Mrs Beaby if it was 'a fac'' that her young Em was leaving her place before her year was up, or Charley's mother if it was true that he and Nell had quarrelled coming home from church last Sunday, and had they made it up, or were they still 'off at hooks', as they called an estrangement.

When Rachel dropped in for a tell, others were sure to follow. Laura, lying on her stomach on the hearth-rug with a picture book propped up before her, or cutting out patterns from paper in a corner, would hear their voices rising and falling or dropping to a whisper when some item they were discussing was not considered suitable for children's ears. She would sometimes long to ask questions, but dare not, for it was a strict rule there that children should be seen, but not heard. It was better not even to laugh when something funny was said, for that might call attention to oneself and some one might say: 'That child's gettin' too knowin'. I hope she ain't goin' to turn out one of them forrard sort, for I can't abide 'em.' At that her mother would bridle and say that, far from being forward, she was rather young for her age, and as to being knowing, she didn't suppose she had heard what was said, but had laughed because they were laughing. At the same time, she took care to send Laura upstairs, or out into the garden for something, when she thought the conversation was taking an unsuitable turn.

Sometimes one of them would let fall a remark about the vague far-distant days before the children were born. 'My ole gran-fer used to say that all the land between here and the church wer' left by will to th' poor o' th' parish in the old times; all common land of turf and fuzz 'twas then; but 'twer' all stole away an' cut up into fields,' and another would agree, 'Yes, so I've allus heard.'

Sometimes one of them would bring out some surprising saying, as Patty Wardup did when the rest of the company were discussing Mrs Eames's fur cape: she couldn't have bought it and it certainly did not grow upon her back, yet she had appeared in it last Sunday at church, and not so much as a word to anybody as to how she had got it. True, as Mrs Baker suggested, it did look something like a coachman's shoulder tippet – dark, thick fur, bearskin, they called it – and she had once said she had a brother who was a coachman somewhere up country. Then Patty, who had been pensively twisting her doorkey between her fingers and taking no part in the conversation, said quietly: 'The golden ball rolls to everybody's feet once in a lifetime. That's what my Uncle Jarvis used to say and I've seen it myself, over and over.'

What golden ball? And who was her Uncle Jarvis? And what had a golden ball to do with Mrs Eames's fur tippet? No wonder they all laughed and said, 'She's dreaming as usual!'

Patty was not a native of those parts, but had come there only a few years before as housekeeper to an elderly man whose wife had died. As was the custom when no relative was available, he had applied to the Board of Guardians for a housekeeper and Patty had been selected as the most suitable inmate of the workhouse at the time. She was a plump little woman with pale brown, satin-sleek hair and mild blue eyes, well set off on her arrival by the bunch of forget-me-nots in her bonnet. How she had come to be in the workhouse was a mystery, for she was still in the forties, able bodied, and evidently belonging to a slightly higher stratum of society than her new employer. She told her story to no one and no one asked her for it. 'Ax no questions and you'll be told no lies, although you may hear a few without axing' was the hamlet motto. But she was generally acknowledged to be 'superior', for did she not plait her hair in fives every day, instead of in threes all the week and in fives on Sunday, and exchange her white apron after dinner for a small black satin one with beaded trimming? She was a good cook, too. Amos was lucky. On the very first Sunday after she arrived she made a meat pudding with a crust so light a puff of wind would have blown it away and with thick, rich gravy that gushed out in a stream when the knife was stuck into it. Old Amos said the very smell made his mouth water and began inquiring how soon after his wife's death it would be decent to put up the banns. It was tacitly understood that such engagements would lead to marriage.

But she did not marry Old Amos. He had a son – Old Amos and Young Amos to the hamlet – and Young Amos got in his proposal first and was accepted. The hamlet women did not hold, as they said, with the wife being older than the husband and Patty was a good ten years older than her intended; but they thought Young

Amos had done well for himself, especially when, immediately before the wedding, a cartload of furniture arrived, together with a trunk of clothes which Patty had somehow managed to save from the wreck of her fortunes and hide up somewhere.

They had already thought Patty was superior and they were sure of it when it became known that the furniture included a feather-bed, a leather-covered couch with chairs to match and a stuffed owl in a glass case. Somehow they learned, or perhaps Young Amos told them, for he was inclined to be boastful, that Patty had been married before – to a publican, if you please! And then to come down to the workhouse, poor thing! But what a mercy she'd had the wit to hide up her good things. If she hadn't, the Guardians would have had them.

Patty and Amos were a model couple when they went to the market town to shop on a Saturday night, Patty in her black silk with flounces, her good Paisley shawl and her ivory-handled umbrella, rolled up in its shiny black macintosh case to preserve the silk cover. But, gradually another side of the picture emerged. Patty was fond of her glass of stout. Nobody blamed her for that, for it was well known she could afford it and she must have been used to it in her public-house days. Presently it was noticed that on their marketing nights Amos and Patty came later and later from town, and then, one sad night, somebody passed them on the road and reported that Patty had had so many glasses of stout, or of something stronger, that it was as much as Amos could do to coax her along. Some said he was carrying her. That accounted for the workhouse, they said, and they waited for Amos to begin beating her. But he never did, nor did he ever mention her weakness or complain about her to anybody.

Her lapses occurred only at week-ends and she was not noisy or quarrelsome, only helpless. The hamlet would be in darkness and most of the people in bed when they stole home silently and Amos carried Patty upstairs. He may even have thought that none of the neighbours knew of his wife's failing. If so, it was a vain hope. It sometimes seemed as if the very hedges had eyes and the road-way ears, for, next morning, the whisper ran round as to which public-house Patty had favoured, the nature and number of her drinks, and how far she had got on her homeward way before her potations overcame her. But if Amos did not mind, why should other folks? 'Twas not as if she'd made a beast of herself in public. So Patty and Amos, with that one reservation, were still looked upon as a model couple.

It was one of the children's treats to be invited into her house to see her stuffed owl and other treasures, which included some pressed flowers from the Holy Land in a frame made of olive wood from the Mount of Olives. Another treasure was a fan made of long white ostrich feathers which she would take out of its case and show them, then fan herself gently as she reclined on her couch with her feet up. 'I've seen better times,' she would say in her more talkative moods. 'Yes, I've seen better times, but I've never seen a better husband than Amos, and I like this little house where I can shut the door and do as I like. After all, a public's never your own. Anybody who's got two pennies to rub together can come in and out as they like, without so much as a knock at the door or a ''by your leave'', and what's grand furniture as isn't your own, for you can't call it that when other people have the use of it.' And she would curl up on her couch and shut her eyes, for, although she was never known to get tipsy at home, her breath sometimes had a queer, sweetish smell which an older person might have recognized as that of gin. 'Now, run along,' she would say, opening one eye; 'and lock the door behind you and put the key on the window-sill. I don't want any more visitors and I'm not going out. This isn't one of my visiting days.'

Then there was a young married woman named Gertie who passed as a beauty, entirely on the strength of a tiny waist and sim- pering smile. She was a great reader of novelettes and had romantic ideas. Before her marriage she had been a housemaid at one of the country mansions where men-servants were kept, and their company and compliments had spoiled her for her kind, honest great cart-horse of a husband. She loved to talk about her conquests, telling of the time Mr Pratt, the butler, had danced with her four times at the servants' ball, and how jealous her John had been. He had been invited for her sake but could not dance, and had sat there all the evening, like a great gowk, in his light-grey Sunday suit, with his great red hands hanging down between his knees, and a chrysanthemum in his buttonhole as big as a pancake.

She had worn her white silk, the one she was afterwards married in, and her hair had been curled by a real hairdresser – the maids had clubbed together to pay for his attendance, and he had afterwards stayed for the dancing and paid special attention to Gertrude. 'And you should've seen our John, his eyes simply rolling with jealousy . . .' But, if she managed to get so far, she was then interrupted. No one wanted to hear about her conquests, but they were willing to hear about the dresses. What did the cook wear? Black lace over a red silk underslip. That sounded handsome. And the head housemaid and the stillroom maid, and so on, down to the tweeny, who, it had to be confessed, could afford nothing more exciting than her best frock of grey cloth.

Gertie was the only one of them all who discussed her relations with her husband. 'I don't think our Johnny loves me any more,' she would sigh. 'He went off to work this morning without kissing me.' Or, 'Our John's getting a regular chaw-bacon. He went to sleep and snored in his chair after tea last night. I felt that lonely I could have cried me eyes out.' And the more robust characters would laugh and ask her what more she expected of a man who had been at work in the fields all day, or say, 'Times is changed, my gal. You ain't courtin' no longer.'

Gertie was a fool and the hamlet laughing-stock for a year or so; then young John arrived and the white silk was cut up to make him a christening robe and Gertie forgot her past triumphs in the more recent one of producing such a paragon. 'Isn't he lovely?' she would say, exhibiting her red, shapeless lump of a son, and those who had been most unsympathetic with her former outpourings would be the first to declare him a marvellous boy. 'He's the very spit of his dad; but he's got your eyes, Gertie. My word! He's going to break some hearts when the time comes, you'll see.' As time went on, Gertie grew red and lumpy herself. Gone were the wasp waist and the waxen pallor she had thought so genteel. But she still managed to keep her romantic ideas, and the last time Laura saw her, by that time a middle-aged woman, she assured her that her daughter's recent marriage to a stable-boy was 'a regular romance in real life', although, as far as her listener could gather, it was what the hamlet people of the preceding generation would have called 'a pushed on, hugger-mugger sort of affair'.

Laura did not like Gertie's face. Her features were not bad, but she had protruding pale blue eyes of which the whites were always faintly bloodshot, and her complexion was of a sickly yellowish shade. Even her small mouth, so much admired by some of the hamlet judges of beauty, was repulsive to a child. It was drawn up so close that the lips made tiny wrinkles, like stitches round a button-hole. 'A mouth like a hen's backside', one rude man said of it.

But there was one visiting neighbour Laura loved to look at, for her face reminded her of that on the cameo brooch her mother used to pin her lace collar on Sundays, and her black hair rippled down from its centre parting as though that also was carved. Her fine head had a slight droop that showed up the line of her neck and shoulders and, although her clothes were no better than those of other people, they looked better on her. She was always in black, for no sooner was the year and a half mourning up for one great-uncle or first or second cousin than another died. Or, failing an actual death, she decided it would not be worth while to 'bring out her colours' with some distant relative over eighty or 'just at the last'. If she knew that black suited her, she was too wise to mention that fact. People would have thought her vain, or peculiar, to wear black for choice, whereas mourning there was no gainsaying.

'Mother,' said Laura one day after this neighbour had gone, 'doesn't Mrs Merton look lovely?'

Her mother laughed. 'Lovely? No. Though some might think her good-looking. She's too pale and melancholy for my taste and her nose is too long.'

Mrs Merton, as Laura remembered her in after years, might have sat for a picture as the Tragic Muse. She was of a melancholy nature. 'I've supped sorrow with a spoon,' she was never tired of saying. 'I've supped sorrow with a spoon and sorrow will always be my lot.' Yet, as the children's mother reminded her, she had little to complain of. She had a good husband and not too large a family. As well as the distant relations, some of whom she had never seen, she had lost one child in infancy and her father had recently died of old age, and the loss of her pig from swine fever two years before was admittedly a serious affliction; but these were losses such as any one might experience. Many had, and yet managed to get over them without talking about supping sorrow.

Does melancholy attract misfortune? Or is it true that past, present and future are one, only divided by our time sense? Mrs Merton was fated to become in her old age the tragic figure she had looked when young. Her husband was already dead when her only son and two grandsons were killed in the 1914–18 War and she was left practically alone in the world.

By that time she had gone to live in another village, and Laura's mother, herself bereaved by the War, walked over to see her and sympathize. She found her a sad but resigned old woman. There was no longer any talk about supping sorrow, no mourning her own woes, but a quiet acceptance of the world as it then was and a resolute attempt at cheerfulness.

It was spring and her room had flowers in pots and vases. The air was rather faint with the scent of them, her visitor noticed; then, looking more closely, she found they were not garden flowers. Every pot and jug and vase was filled with hawthorn blossom.

She was rather shocked at this, for, although less superstitious than many countrywomen, she herself would not have brought may blossom indoors. It might be unlucky, or it might not, but there was no sense in running unnecessary risks.

'Aren't you afraid all this may'll bring you bad luck?' she asked Mrs Merton as they sipped their tea.

Mrs Merton smiled, and a smile from her was almost as unusual as to see may indoors. 'How can it?' she said. 'I've got nobody else to lose. I've always been fond of those flowers. So I thought I'd bring some of them in and enjoy them. My thread's spun as far as luck's concerned.'

Politics were seldom mentioned by the women. If they did come up it was usually by way of comment on some husband's excessive zeal. 'Why can't he leave such things alone? 'Tis no business of his'n,' some wife would say. 'What does it matter to him who governs? Whoever 'tis, they won't give us nothing, and they can't take nothing away from us, for you can't get blood from a stone.'

Some would discriminate and say it was a pity the men had taken up with these Liberal notions. 'If they've got to vote, why not vote Tory and keep in with the gentry? You never hear of Liberals giving the poor a bit of coal or a blanket at Christmas.' As, indeed, you did not, for there was no Liberal in the parish but bought his own coals by the hundredweight and might think himself lucky if his wife had a blanket for each bed.

A few of the older men were equally poor-spirited. One election day the children, coming home from school, met an old, semi-bedridden neighbour, riding, propped up with cushions, in a luxurious carriage to the polling station. A few days afterwards, when Laura had taken him some small delicacy from her mother, he whispered to her at parting: 'Tell y're dad I voted Liberal. He! He! They took th' poor old hoss to th' water, but he didn't drink out o' their trough. Not he!'

When Laura gave her father the message he did not seem as pleased as their neighbour had expected. He said he thought it was 'a bit low down to roll up in anybody's carriage to vote against them'; but her mother laughed and said: 'Serves 'em right for dragging the poor old hunks out of bed in that weather.'

Apart from politics, the hamlet people's attitude towards those they called 'the gentry' was peculiar. They took a pride in their rich and powerful country-house neighbours, especially when titled. The old Earl in the next parish was spoken of as 'our Earl' and when the flag, flown from the tower of his mansion to show he was in residence, could be seen floating above tree-tops they would say: 'I see our family's at home again.'

They sometimes saw him pass through the hamlet in his carriage, an old, old man, sunk deep in cushions and half-buried in rugs, often too comatose to be aware of, or acknowledge, their curtsies. He had never spoken to them or given them anything, for they did not live in his cottages, and in the way of Christmas coals and blankets he had his own parish to attend to; but the men worked on his land, though not directly employed by him, and by some inherited instinct they felt he belonged to them.

For wealth without rank or birth they had small respect. When a rich retired hatter bought a neighbouring estate and set up as a country gentleman, the hamlet was scandalized. 'Who's he?' they said. 'Only a shopkeeper pretending to be gentry. I 'udn't work for him, no, not if he paid me in gold!' One man who had been sent to clean out a well in his stable-yard and had seen him, said: 'I'd a good mind to ask him to sell me a hat'; and that was repeated for weeks as a great joke. Laura was told in after years that their better-educated neighbours were almost as prejudiced; they did not call on the newly rich family. That was before the days when a golden key could open any door.

Landowners of established rank and stern or kindly J.P.s and their ladies were respected. Some of the sons or grandsons of local families were said to be 'wild young devils' and were looked upon with a kind of horrified admiration. The tradition of the Hell-fire Club had not entirely faded, and one young nobleman was reputed to have 'gambled away' one of his family estates at one sitting. There were hints of more lurid orgies in which a bunch of good-looking country girls were supposed to figure, and a saintly curate, an old white-haired man, went to admonish the young spark, at that time living alone in a wing of the otherwise deserted family mansion. There was no record of the conversation, but the result was known. The older man was pushed or kicked down the front door flight of steps and the door was banged and bolted against him. Then, the story went, he raised himself to his knees and prayed aloud for 'the poor sinful child' within. The gardener, greatly daring, supported him to his cottage and made him rest before attempting to walk home.

But the great majority of the country gentlepeople lived decent, if, according to hamlet standards, not particularly useful lives. In summer the carriage was at the door at three o'clock in the afternoon to take the lady of the house and her grown-up daughters, if any, to pay calls. If they found no one in, they left cards, turned down at the corner, or not turned down, according to etiquette. Or they stayed at home to receive their own callers and played croquet and drank tea under spreading cedars on exquisitely kept lawns. In winter they hunted with the local pack; and, summer and winter, they never failed to attend Sunday morning service at their parish church. They had always a smile and a nod for their poorer neighbours who saluted them, with more substantial favours for those who lived in the cottages on their estates. As to their inner lives, the commonalty knew no more than the Britons knew of the Romans who inhabited the villas dotted about the countryside; and it is doubtful if the county families knew more of their poorer neighbours than the Romans did of theirs, in spite of speaking the same language.

Here and there the barrier of caste was overstepped. Perhaps by some young man or girl who, in advance of their time, realized that the population beyond their park gates were less 'the poor' in a lump than individual men and women who happened to have been born to poverty. Of such it was sometimes said: 'He's different, Master Raymond is; you can say anything to him, he's more like one of ourselves than one of the gentry. Makes you split your sides, he does, with some of his tales, and he's got a feeling heart, too, and don't button his pockets too tight. Good thing if there were more like him.' Or: 'Miss Dorothy, now, she's different. No asking questions and questions when she comes to see anybody; but she sets her down and if you've a mind to tell her anything, you can and know it won't go no further. I 'udn't mind seeing her come in when I was in the godspeed of washday, and that's saying something.'

On the other hand, there were old nurses and trusted maids who had come to be regarded as individuals and loved as true friends, irrespective of class, by those they served. And the name of 'friend', when applied to them in words, gave them a deeper satisfaction than any material benefit. A retired lady's maid, whom Laura knew later, spoke to her many times with much feeling of what she evidently regarded as the crown of her experiences. She had been for many years maid to a titled lady moving in high society, had dressed her for royal courts, undressed and put her to bed in illness, travelled with her, indulged her innocent vanities, and knew, for she could not help knowing, being so near her person, her most intimate griefs. At last 'Her Ladyship', grown old, lay upon her deathbed and her maid, who was helping to nurse her, happened to be alone in the room with her, her relatives, none of whom were very near ones, being downstairs at dinner. ' "Raise me up," she said, and I raised her up, and when she put her arms round my neck to help lift her, she kissed me and said, *"My friend,"* ' and Miss Wilson, twenty years after, considered that kiss and those two words a more ample reward for her years of devotion than the nice cottage and annuity she received under the will of the poor lady.

V

Mrs Herring

When Laura said she had seen a ghost coming out of the clothes closet in the bedroom she had not meant to tell a lie. She really believed she had seen one. One evening, before it was quite dark and yet the corners of the room were shadowy her mother had sent her upstairs to fetch something out of the chest, and, as she leant over it, with one eye turned apprehensively towards the clothes closet corner, she thought she saw something move. At the time she felt sure she saw something move, though she had no clear idea of what it was that was moving. It may have been a lock of her own hair, or the end of a window-curtain stirring, or merely a shadow seen sideways; but, whatever it was, it was sufficient to send her screaming and stumbling downstairs.

At first, her mother was sorry for her, for she thought she had fallen down a step or two and hurt herself; but when Laura said that she had seen a ghost she put her off her lap and began to ask questions.

At that point the fibbing began. When asked what the ghost was like, she first said it was dark and shaggy, like a bear; then that it was tall and white, adding as an after-thought that it had eyes like lanterns and she thought it was carrying one, but was not sure. 'I don't suppose you are sure,' said her mother dryly. 'If you ask me, it's all a parcel of fibs, and if you don't look out you'll be struck dead, like Ananias and Sapphira in the Bible,' and she proceeded to tell their story as a warning.

After that, Laura never spoke of the closet to any one else but Edmund; but she was still desperately afraid of it, as she had been as long as she could remember. There was something terrifying

46

about a door which was never unlocked, and a door in such a dark corner. Even her mother had never seen inside it, for the contents belonged to their landlady, Mrs Herring, who when she moved out of the house had left some of her belongings there, saying she would fetch them as soon as possible. 'What was inside it?' the children used to ask each other. Edmund thought there was a skeleton, for he had heard his mother say, 'There's a skeleton in every cupboard,' but Laura felt it was nothing as harmless.

After they were in bed and their mother had gone downstairs at night, she would turn her back on the door, but, if she peeped round, as she often did – for how otherwise could she be sure that it was not slowly opening? – all the darkness in the room seemed to be piled up in that corner. There was the window, a grey square, with sometimes a star or two showing, and there were the faint outlines of the chair and the chest, but where the closet door should have been was only darkness.

'Afraid of a locked door!' her mother exclaimed one night when she found her sitting up in bed and shivering. 'What's inside it? Only a lot of old lumber, you may be sure. If there was anything much good, she'd have fetched it before now. Lie down and go to sleep, do, and don't be silly!' *Lumber! Lumber!* What a queer word, especially when said over and over beneath the bedclothes. It meant odds and ends of old rubbish, her mother had explained, but, to her, it sounded more like black shadows come alive and ready to bear down on one.

Her parents disliked the closet, too. They paid the rent of the house and did not see why even a small part of it should be reserved for the landlady's use; and, until the closet was cleared, they could not carry out their plan of removing the front, throwing the extra space into the room, and then running up a wooden partition to make a small separate bedroom for Edmund. So her father wrote to Mrs Herring, and one day she arrived and turned out to be a little, lean old lady with a dark brown mole on one leathery cheek and wearing a black bonnet decorated with jet dangles, like tiny fishing rods. The children's mother had asked her when she arrived if she would not like to take off her bonnet, but she had said she could not, for she had not brought her cap; and, to make it look less formal for indoor wear, she had untied the ribbon bow beneath her chin and flung a bonnet string over each shoulder. Thus unmoored, the bonnet had grown more and more askew, which went oddly with her genteel manner.

Edmund and Laura sat on the bed and watched her shake out old garments and examine them for moth holes and blow the dust off crockery with her bellows which she had borrowed, until the air of the clean, bright room was as thick with dust as that of a lime kiln. 'Plenty of dust!' their mother said, wrinkling her pretty nose distastefully. But Mrs Herring did nothing to abate it. Why should she? She was in her own house; her tenants were privileged to be allowed to live there. At least that was what Laura read in the upward movement of her little pointed nose.

Now that the closet door was thrown back it revealed a deep, whitewashed den going back to the eaves of the cottage. It was crammed with the hoarding of years, with old clothes and shoes, legless chairs, empty picture frames, handleless cups and spoutless teapots. The best things had gone downstairs already; the lace-pillow on a stand, the huge green gig umbrella with whalebone ribs, and the nest of copper preserving pans that Laura's mother said afterwards were worth a mint of money. From the window, Mr Herring could be seen arranging them in the spring cart, his thin legs straddling in drab gaiters. There would not be room in the cart for everything, and the hire of it for the day was too costly to make another journey possible. The time had come for Mrs Herring to decide what was best worth taking.

'I wonder what I'd better do,' she kept saying to the children's mother, but she got no helpful suggestions from one who detested what she called 'a lot of old clutter laid up in dark corners'.

'She's an old hoarder. A regular old hoarder!' she whispered to Laura when Mrs Herring had gone downstairs to consult her husband. 'And don't let me see you mess with that old rubbish she's given you. Put it down, and when she's gone it can be cleaned or burnt.' They put down their presents reluctantly. Edmund had been pleased with his broken corkscrew and coil of short lengths of string, and Laura had admired her flannel-leaved needlebook with 'Be Diligent' worked in cross-stitch on its canvas cover. The needles inside were all rusty, but that did not matter; it was as a work of art she valued it. But before they had time to protest, Mrs Herring's head appeared round the banisters, her bonnet more than ever askew by that time and her face smutted by cobwebs. 'Would these be any good to you, my dear?' she asked, handing down a coil of light steel hoops from a nail in the wall of the closet.

'It's very kind of you, I'm sure,' was the guarded response; 'but, somehow, I don't see myself wearing a crinoline again.'

'No. Right out of fashion,' Mrs Herring admitted. 'Pity, too, for it was a handy fashion for young married women. I've known some, wearing a good-sized crinoline, go right up to the day of their confinement without so much as their next-door neighbour suspecting. Now look at the brazen trollops! And here's a lovely picture of the Prince Consort, and that's somebody you've never heard of, I'll lay,' turning to the children.

Oh, yes, they had. Their mother had told them that when the Prince Consort died every lady in the land had gone into mourning, and, no matter how often they were told this, they always asked, 'And did you go into mourning, too, Mother?' and were told that she had been only a girl at the time, but she had had a black sash and ribbons. And they knew he had been the Queen's husband, though, oddly enough, not the King, and that he had been so good that nobody had liked him in his lifetime, excepting the Queen, who 'fairly doted'. They had heard all this by degrees because a neighbour called 'Old Queenie' had portraits of him and the Queen on the lid of her snuffbox.

But Mrs Herring was back in the closet and, since she could not take all her things away with her, was determined to be generous. 'Now, here's a nice little beaded footstool. Come out of Tusmore House that time the fire was, so you may be sure it's good. You have it, my dear. I'd like you to have it.' Their mother eyed the little round stool with the claw legs and beaded cover. She would really have liked that, but had made up her mind to accept nothing. Perhaps she reflected, too, that it would be hers in any case, as what

Mrs Herring could not take she would have to leave, for she said again: 'It's very kind of you, I'm sure, but I don't know that I've any use for it.'

'Use! Use!' echoed Mrs Herring. 'Keep a thing seven years and you'll always find a use for it! Besides,' she added, rather sharply, 'it's just the thing to have under your feet when you're suckling, and you can't pretend you'll not be doing that again, *and* a good many times, too, at your age.'

Fortunately, at that moment, Mr Herring was heard calling upstairs that the cart was so chock-a-block that he couldn't get so much as another needle in edgeways, and, with a deep sigh his wife said she supposed she'd have to leave the rest. 'Perhaps you could sell some of the best things and send the money on with the rent,' she suggested hopefully, but the children's mother thought a bonfire in the garden would be the best way of disposing of them. However, after she had gone, a number of things were picked out and cleaned and kept, including the beaded footstool, a brass ladle, and a little travelling clock, which, when repaired, delighted the children by playing a little tune after striking the hours. 'Tinkle, tinkle, tinkle, tink, tink, tink' it went, night and day, for another forty years! then, its works worn out at last, retired to a shelf in Laura's attic.

Downstairs, the table was laid with a 'visitor's tea'. There were the best tea things with a fat pink rose on the side of each cup; hearts of lettuce, thin bread and butter, and the crisp little cakes that had been baked in readiness that morning. Edmund and Laura sat very upright in their hard windsor chairs. Bread and butter first. Always bread and butter first: they had been told that so many times that it had the finality of a text of Scripture. But Mr Herring, who was the eldest present and ought to have set a good example, began with the little cakes, picking up and examining each one closely before disposing of it in two bites. However, while there were still a few left, Mrs Herring placed bread and butter on his plate and handed him the lettuce meaningly; and when he twisted the tender young hearts of lettuce into tight rolls and dipped them into the salt-cellar she took the spoon and put salt on the side of his plate.

Mrs Herring ate very genteelly, crumbling her cake on her plate and picking out and putting aside the currants, because, she explained, they did not agree with her. She crooked the little finger of the hand which held her teacup and sipped its contents like a bird, with her eyes turned up to the ceiling.

While they sat there, the door wide open, with the scent of flowers and the humming of bees and the waving of fruit-tree tops seeming to the children to say that the stiff, formal tea-drinking would soon be over and that they were all waiting for them in the garden, a woman paused at the gate, looked the spring cart well over, set down her water-buckets and opened the gate. 'Why, it's Rachel. Whatever can she want?' said the children's mother, rather vexed at the intrusion. What Rachel wanted was to know who the visitors were and why they had come.

'Why, if it ain't Mrs Herring – and Mr Herring, too!' she cried in a tone of joyful recognition as she reached the door. 'An' you've come to clear out that old closet of yours, I'll be bound. I thought to meself when I saw the spring cart at th' gate, "That's Mrs Herring come to fetch away her old lumber at last." But I weren't quite sure, because you've got that waterproof cover over it all. How be ye both, and how do ye like it up yonder?'

During this speech Mrs Herring had frozen visibly. 'We are well, thank you,' she said, 'and we like our present residence very much, though what business it is of yours to inquire, I *don't* know.'

'Oh, no offence intended, no offence,' said Rachel, somewhat abashed. 'I only come to inquire, just friendly like,' and off she stumped down the path, throwing another inquisitive glance at the cart as she passed it.

'There! Did you ever!' Mrs Herring exclaimed. 'I never saw such a lot of heathen Turks in my life! A woman I took good care barely to pass the time of day with when I lived here to come hail-fellow-well-metting me like that!'

'She didn't mean any harm,' apologized Laura's mother. 'There's so little going on here that when anybody does come the folks take more interest than they would in a town.'

'I'd interest her! I'd hail-fellow-well-met her!' exclaimed Mr

Herring, who had so far sat mute. 'I'd teach her how to behave to her betters, if I had my way.'

'God knows I did my best to put them in their places when we were living here,' sighed Mrs Herring, her anger subsiding, 'but 'twas no good. Why we ever thought to live in such a place I couldn't tell you if you asked me, unless it was that the house was going cheap at the time Mr Herring retired and a nice bit of ground went with it. It's very different at Candleford. Of course, there are poor people there, but we don't have to associate with them; they keep to their part of the town and we keep to ours. You should see our house: nice iron railings in front and an entry where the stairs go up, not like this, with the door opening straight out on the path and anybody right on top of you before you know where you are. Not but what this is a nice little house,' she added hastily, remembering that she owned it, 'but you know what I mean. Candleford's different. Civilized, that's what my son-in-law calls it, and he works at the biggest grocer's in the town, so he ought to know. It's civilized, he says, and he's right. You can't call a place like this civilized, now can you?'

Laura thought it must be a fine thing to be civilized until, later, she asked her mother what the word meant and her mother replied: 'A civilized place is where the people wear clothes and don't run naked like savages.' So it meant nothing, for everybody in this country wore clothes. One old Lark Rise woman wore three flannel petticoats in winter. She thought that if all the Candleford people were like Mr and Mrs Herring she would not like them much. How rude they had been to poor Rachel!

But they were funny. When her father came home from work that night her mother told him about the visit, imitating first Mrs Herring's voice, then that of Mr Herring, and making the one even more carefully genteel than it had been and the other more sudden and squeaky.

They all laughed a good deal, then her father said: 'I forgot to tell you I saw Harris last night and he says we can have the pony and cart any Sunday we like now.'

The children were so pleased they made a little song about it:

We're going over to Candleford,
   To Candleford, to Candleford,
We're going over to Candleford
   To see our relations,

and they sang it about the house so often that their mother said it just about drove her melancholy mad. The loan of the pony and cart was not everything, it appeared; the half-year's rent had to be got together and taken because, big as Candleford was, the Herrings would know they had been. They knew everything, nosy parkers as they were, and if the rent, then about due, was not taken, they would think their tenants had not the money. That would never do. 'Don't be poor and look poor, too,' was a family maxim. Then the Sunday outfits had to be overhauled and a few small presents purchased to take with them. Planning a summer Sunday outing in those days meant more than turning over the leaves of a bus time-table.

VI

Over to Candleford

Very early one Sunday morning, while the rest of the hamlet was still asleep and the sky was still pink and the garden flowers and currant bushes were still greyish-rough with dew, they heard the sounds of wheels drawing up at their gate and knew that the innkeeper's old pony had come with the spring cart to take them.

Father and Mother rode on the front seat, Father in his best black coat and grey-striped trousers and Mother resplendent in her pale grey wedding gown with rows and rows of narrow blue velvet ribbon edging its many flounces. The wedding bonnet had long been cast aside, for, as she often said, 'headgear does date so', and on this occasion she wore a tiny blue velvet bonnet, like a little flat mat on her hair, with wide velvet strings tied in a bow under her chin, – a new bonnet, the procuring of which had helped to delay the expedition. Upon her lap she nursed a basket containing the presents; a bottle of her elderberry wine, a fowl she had specially fattened, and a length of pillow-lace, made to order by a neighbour, which she thought would make nice neckfrills for the cousins' best frocks. Their father, not to be outdone in generosity, at the last moment filled the back of the cart, where Edmund and Laura were to sit, with a selection of his choicest vegetables, so that, throughout the drive, Laura's legs rested higher than her seat on a sack of spring cabbage, the first of the season.

At last the children were strapped into the high, narrow seat with their backs to those of their parents and off they went, their father coaxing the old grey mare past her stable door, which she made determined efforts to enter, with: 'Come on, Polly, old girl. Not tired already. Why, we haven't started yet.' Later on, he lost patience and called her 'a measley old screw', and once, when she stopped dead in the middle of the road, he said, 'Damn the mare!' and their mother looked back over the shoulder as though she feared the animal's owner might hear. Between the stops, she trotted in little bursts, and the children bumped up and down in their seat like rubber balls bouncing. All of which was as exciting to them as a flight in an aeroplane would be to a modern child.

From their high seat they could see over hedges into buttercup meadows where cows lay munching the wet grass and big cropping cart-horses loomed up out of the morning mist. In one place the first wild roses were out in the hedge and their father lassoed a spray with his whip and passed it over his shoulder to Laura. The delicate pale pink cups had dew in them. Farther on, he stopped Polly, handed the reins to their mother and leapt down. 'Ah! I thought so!' he said as he plunged his arm into the hedge at a spot from which he had seen a bird flutter out, and he came back with two bright blue eggs in his palm and let them all feel and stroke them before putting them back in the nest. They were warm and as soft as satin.

'Pat, pat, pat', went Polly's hooves in the dust, 'creak, creak, creak', went the harness, and 'rattle, rattle, rattle', went the iron-tyred wheels over the stony places. The road might have been made entirely for their convenience. There was no other vehicle upon it. The farm carts and bakers' vans which passed that way on week-days were standing in yards with their shafts pointing skyward; the gentry's carriages reposed in lofty, stone-paved coach-houses, and coachmen and carters and drivers were all still in bed, for it was Sunday.

The blinds of roadside cottages were drawn and their gardens were deserted of all but a prowling cat or a thrush cracking a snail on a stone, and the children bumped and jolted on through this early morning world with their hearts full of blissful expectation.

They were going over to Candleford. It was always called 'going over', for the country people never spoke of just plain going anywhere; it had to be going up or down or round or over to a place, and there were so many ups and downs, so many small streams to cross and so many gates across roads to open between their home and Candleford that 'going over' seemed best to describe the journey.

Towards midday they passed through a village where the people, in their Sunday best, were streaming towards the lych-gate of the church. The squire and the farmers wore top hats, and the squire's head gardener and the schoolmaster and the village carpenter. The farm labourers wore bowlers, or, the older men, soft, round black felts. With the top-hatted men were women in rich, dark, heavy dresses who clung to their husbands' arms while their children walked meekly in front or, not so meekly, behind them. Other villagers in work-day clothes, with very clean shirts and their boots unlaced for greater Sunday ease, carried their dinners to the baker's, or stood in a group at the bakehouse door; while slowly up and down the road in front of them paced a handsome pair of greys with a carriage behind them and a coachman and a footman on the box with cockades in their glossy hats. Shepherded by their teachers, the schoolchildren marched two and two to church from the Sunday School.

This village was so populous and looked so fine, with its pretty cottages standing back on each side of an avenue of young chestnut trees, that Laura thought at first it was Candleford. But, no, she was told; it was Lord So-and-So's place. No doubt the carriage and greys belonged to him. It was what was called a model village, with three bedrooms to every house and a pump to supply water to each group of cottages.

Only good people were allowed to live there, her father said. That was why so many were going to church. He seemed to speak seriously, but her mother clicked her tongue, and, to placate her, he said that he thought the bakehouse was a good idea. 'How would you like to send your Sunday joint out to be baked and find it just done to a turn when you came out of church?' he asked their mother. But that did not seem to please her either; she said more went to the cooking of a good dinner than just baking the meat, and, besides, how could you be sure of getting all your dripping? It was a funny thing bakers so often had dripping to sell. They said they bought it from the cooks at big houses. But did they?

Soon after the model village was left behind Polly got tired and stood stockstill in the road, and their mother suggested a rest and a nosebag for her and some food for them. So they all got out and sat on a stone-heap like gipsies and ate little cakes and drank milk out of a bottle while they listened to the skylarks overhead and smelt the wild thyme at their feet. They were in a new country by then, a country of large grass fields dotted with trees where herds of bullocks grazed, or peered at them through the iron railings by the roadside. Their father pointed out some earthworks, which he said were thrown up by the Romans and described those old warriors in their brass helmets so well that the children seemed to see them; but neither he, nor they, dreamed that another field within sight would one day be surrounded by buildings called 'hangars', or that one day, within their own lifetimes, other warriors would soar from it into the sky, armed with more deadly weapons than the Romans ever knew. No, that field lay dreaming in the sunshine, flat and green, waiting for a future of which they knew nothing.

Soon after that Candleford came out to meet them. First, wayside cottages embowered in flower gardens, then cottages in pairs with iron railings enclosing neat little front plots and tiled paths leading up to the doors. Then the gasometer (for they actually had gas at Candleford!) and the railway station, which made the town accessible to all but such cross-country districts as theirs. Then came pavements and lamp-posts and people, more people than they had ever seen together in their lives before. But, while they were still on the outskirts, they felt their mother nudge their father's arm and heard her ejaculate: 'There's pomp for you! Feathers, if you please!' Then, throwing her voice ahead: 'Why, it's Ethel and Alma, coming to meet us. Here are your cousins. Turn round and wave to them, dears!' Still held by the strap, Laura wriggled round and saw, coming towards them, two tall girls in white.

The feathers that had shocked her mother, partly, perhaps, because of the contrast between their richness and Laura's plain little hat of white chip with its pink ribbon tied round in a bow to match her pink frock, were long white ostrich plumes wreathed round floppy leghorn hats. The hats were exactly alike and the feathers of the same fullness down to the last strand. The white embroidered muslin dresses they wore were also replicas of each other, for it was the fashion then to dress sisters alike, regardless of type. But the girls had seen them and came running towards the spring cart with a twinkle of long, black-stockinged legs and shiny patent-leather best shoes. After the health of themselves, their parents, and the rest of the family had been inquired into, they came round to the back of the cart.

'So this is Laura? And this is dear little Edmund? How do you do? How do you do, dear?' Alma was twelve and Ethel thirteen, but their cool, grown-up manner might have belonged to twenty-five and thirty. Laura began to wish herself back at home as, one blush of embarrassment all over, she answered for herself and Edmund. She could scarcely believe that these two tall, well-dressed, nearly grown-up girls were her cousins. She had expected something quite different.

However, things were easier when their equipage moved on, with Ethel and Alma holding on, one on each side of the tail board, and smiling a little as they answered their uncle's shouted questions. 'Yes, Uncle,' Alma was still at the Candleford school; but Ethel was at Miss Bussell's, a weekly boarder; she came home on Friday night and went back on Monday morning. She was going to stay there until she was old enough to go to the Training College for Schoolteachers. 'That's right!' called Laura's father. 'Stuff your own brains now and you'll be able to stuff other people's hereafter. And Alma, is she going to be a teacher, too?' Oh, no, when she left school she was going to be apprenticed to a Court dressmaker in Oxford. 'That's first rate,' said their uncle. 'Then when Laura is presented at Court she'll be able to make her dress for her.' The girls laughed uncertainly, as if they were not sure if that was meant for a joke or not, and his wife told him not to be 'a great donkey', but Laura felt uncomfortable. The only Court she had heard of was the County Court, to which a neighbour had recently been summoned, and the idea of being presented there was far from pleasant.

It had been arranged that the Lark Rise family should have dinner

at Ethel and Alma's home, not because her parents happened to be
the most prosperous of their Candleford kin, but because their house
came first as they entered the town. Afterwards they were to go on
to see another family of cousins. Laura thought her mother would
have preferred to go there at once, for, when their arrangements
had been discussed at home, she had said something about hating a
lot of fuss and show-off, and that money wasn't everything, though
some folks who had plenty might think so. 'But,' she had concluded,
'they are your relations, not mine, and I expect you understand
them better than I do. But, for goodness' sake, don't get on to
politics with James, like you did at our wedding. If you two talked
till you were black in the face you'd never agree, so what's the good
of arguing'; and her husband had promised, quite meekly for him,
that he would not be the first to bring up the subject.

Candleford seemed a very large and grand place to Laura, with
its several streets meeting in a square where there were many large
shop windows, with the blinds drawn because it was Sunday, and a
doctor's house with a red lamp over the gate, and a church with a
tall spire, and women and girls in light summer frocks and men in
smart suits and white straw, boater-shaped hats.

But they were pulling up at a tall white house set back on a little
green with a chestnut tree supporting scaffold poles and ladders and
a sign which informed the public that James Dowland, Builder and
Contractor, was ready and competent to undertake 'Constructions,
Renovations, and Sanitary Work. Estimates Free'.

Readers have no doubt noticed how seldom builders live in
houses of their own construction. You will find a town or village
expanding in all directions with their masterpieces of modernity in
the way of houses and bungalows; but the builder himself you will
usually find living nearer the heart of things, snugly and comfortably
housed in some more substantial, if less convenient, building of less
recent date. Uncle James Dowland's house was probably Georgian.
The eight windows with their clinging wreaths of wistaria were
beautifully spaced and the flight of steps which led up to the hooded
front door was guarded by the low white posts and chains which
enclosed the little green. But, before Laura could get more than a

general impression and think 'what a nice house', she was in the comfortable arms of her Aunt Edith, who was sure they were all tired out after that long drive in the hot sun and would be glad to rest, and Uncle would be here soon. He was a Churchwarden now and had to attend the morning service; and if Robert would take the horse and cart round to the yard gate – 'You haven't forgotten the way, Robert?' – Alma would call the boy to see to the pony. 'He comes in for an hour or two on Sunday mornings to clean the boots and the knives, you know, Emmie, and I've kept him on today on purpose. Now, you come upstairs with me and I'll find some lotion for Laura's freckles; then you must all have a glass of wine to refresh you. It's all of my own making, so you need not be afraid of it for the children. James would never allow intoxicating liquor in this house.'

The inside of the house seemed like a palace to Laura, after their own homely cottage. There were two parlours, one on each side of the front door, and in one of them a table was spread with decanters and wineglasses and dishes of cakes and fruit and biscuits. 'What a lovely dinner,' Laura whispered to her mother when they happened to be alone in the room for a moment.

'That's not dinner. It's refreshments,' she whispered back, and Laura thought 'refreshments' meant an extra nice dinner provided on such occasions. Then her father and Edmund came back from their hand-washing, Edmund bubbling over with some tale of a chain you could pull which brought water pouring down, 'More water than there is in the brook at home,' and their mother said, 'S-s-hush!' and added that she would explain later. Laura had not seen this marvel. She and her mother had taken off their hats and washed their hands in the best bedroom, a magnificent room with a four-poster bed with green curtains and a double washstand with a jug and basin each for them. 'You'll find the commode in that corner,' her auntie had said, and the commode turned out to be a kind of throne with carpeted steps and a lid which opened. But Laura was older than Edmund and knew it was rude to mention such things.

Uncle James Dowland now came in. He was a big man and an

important-looking one, and seemed to fill even that large, well-proportioned room with his presence. At his approach Aunt Edith's stream of good-natured chatter ran dry, and Alma, who had been tiptoeing round the table, helping herself to a little from most of the dishes, sank down on the couch and pulled her short skirt over her knees. After she had been greeted by a heavy pat on the head, Laura shrank back behind her mother. Uncle James was so tall and stout and dark, with eyebrows so bushy and so thick a moustache, with so glossy a Sunday suit and so heavy a gold watchchain that, before him, the others present seemed to fade into the background. Except Laura's father, who nearly as tall as he was, though slighter, stood with him on the hearthrug, talking about their trade. It turned out afterwards to be the only safe subject.

Uncle James Dowland was one of those leading spirits found at that time in every country town or large village. In addition to attending to his own not inconsiderable business of building new houses, renovating old ones, and keeping everybody's roofs and drains in order, he was People's Churchwarden, choirman, and occasional organist, a member of every committee, and auditor of all charity accounts. But his chief interest was in the temperance movement, at that time a regular feature of parochial life. His hatred of intoxicating drink amounted to a phobia, and he used to say that if he saw a workman of his entering a public-house, he would not be his workman much longer. But he was not content with ruling his own home and business in this respect; the whole town was his mission field, and if he could coax or bribe some unhappy workman into signing away his nightly half-pint he became as exhilarated as if his tender for building a mansion had been accepted.

To him the smallest child was worth winning as a temperance convert. He would guide their tiny hands as they signed the temperance pledge, and to keep them in the fold he had established a Band of Hope which met once a week to eat buns and drink lemonade at his expense and to sing to his accompaniment on the school harmonium such rousing ditties as 'Pray sell no more drink to my father' or:

Father, dear Father, come home with me now,
  The clock in the steeple strikes one.
You promised, dear Father, that you would come home
  As soon as your day's work was done

while, all the time, their own excellent fathers, after a modest half-pint at their favourite inn, were already at home and the singers themselves were likely to get into trouble for being out late.

Edmund and Laura, that first Sunday, wrote their names on a handsome blue-and-gold illuminated pledge card, thereby promising they would henceforth touch no intoxicating liquor, 'so help me God'. They were not quite sure what intoxicating liquor was, but they liked the cards and were pleased when their uncle offered to have them framed to hang over their beds at home.

Their Aunt Edith was more attractive to children. She was pink and plump and had wavy grey hair and kind grey eyes. She was dressed in grey silk and when she stirred there was a faint scent of lavender. She looked kind and was kind; but, that discovered and acknowledged, there was little more to be said about her. Away from her husband and daughters she was talkative, running on from subject to subject, like a brook babbling. She greatly admired her husband, and every moment when alone with Laura's mother was devoted to his praise. It was James says this, and James did that, and stories to show how important and respected he was. In his presence she seemed a little afraid of him and she was certainly afraid of her daughters. It was 'What do you think, dear?' or 'What would you do if you were me?' to the girls before she would express an opinion or make an arrangement. Then, to her sister-in-law, 'Of course, you see, Emmie, they've got different ideas to us, with all this education and getting to know people.' She had already informed her that they sometimes played tennis at the Rectory.

Laura thought the girls were conceited, and, although she could not have put it into words, felt they patronized her mother and her as poor relations; but perhaps she was wrong. It may only have been that they were so far removed in circumstances and interests that they had nothing in common. That was the only time Laura was to meet them upon anything like equal terms. They were away from home at the time of her next visit and grown-up before she saw them again. She was only just in time to catch the last flick of their skirts as they began to climb the social ladder which would take them right out of her own life.

The dinner which speedily followed the refreshments was superlative. At one end of the table was a leg of lamb, roasted before an open fire to conserve the juices; at the other a couple of boiled fowls garnished with slices of ham. There were jellies and cheese-cakes, and gooseberry tart with cream.

'The girl' brought in and cleared away the dishes. The maid in a tradesman's family was then always known as 'the girl', irrespective of age. In this case she was a girl of about fifty, who had been with Aunt Edith from the day she was married and was to remain with her as long as she lived. According to Laura's mother, she was overworked, but, if so, it appeared to agree with her, for she was rosy and round as a tub, and the only complaint she was ever known to make was that 'the Missis' would always make the pastry herself, although she knew that she (Bertha) had a lighter hand with a rolling-pin. She kept the whole of the fair-sized house cleaned and polished and whitestoned, helped the washer-woman on Mondays, cooked the meals, and mended the stockings, and all for twelve pounds a year. She was kind, too. Seeing on that first visit Laura had no appetite for dinner after the refreshments, she whisked her scarcely touched plate away while the others were talking.

It was all very rich and fine, but frightfully dull to a child who had come with such high expectations. They were back in the first parlour. The refreshments had disappeared and there was a green plush cloth on the table. Ethel and Alma had gone to Sunday School, where both took classes, and Laura had been given a book with views of Ramsgate to look at. The window blinds were drawn, for the sun was hot on the panes, and the room smelt of best clothes, furniture polish, and potpourri. Edmund was already asleep on his mother's knee and Laura was getting drowsy when the soft buzz of grown-up conversation which had been going on over her head was broken by sharp cries of 'Ireland', 'Home Rule', 'Gladstone says . . .'

Flora Thompson

'Lord Harrington says . . .' 'Joey Chamberlain says . . .' The two men had got on to the subject which her mother had dreaded.

'They're subjects of Queen Victoria, ain't they, same as we are,' her uncle insisted. 'Well, then, let 'em behave as such and be thankful to have a decent Government over 'em. Nice thing they'd make of governing themselves, and they no better than a lot of drunken savages.'

'How'd you like it if a foreign country invaded England . . .' her father began.

'I'd like to see 'em try it,' interposed her uncle.

'. . . invaded England and shed blood like water and burnt down your house and workshops and interfered with your religion. You'd want to get rid of 'em, I'll bet, and get back your independence.'

'Well, we did conquer 'em, didn't we? So let 'em learn who's their masters, I say, and if they won't toe the line, let our soldiers go over and make them.'

'How many Irishmen have you ever known personally?'

'If I'd only known one it'd be one too many; but, as a matter of fact, I've had several working for me at different times. Then there was Colonel Dimmock at Bradley, went bankrupt and let me in for more money than you're ever likely to earn.'

'Now, Bob!' pleaded Laura's mother.

'Now, James!' urged her aunt. 'You're not at a meeting now, but at home, and it's Sunday. What's Ireland to either of you. You've never been there and are never likely to, so have done with your arguing.'

Both men laughed a little and seemed ashamed of their vehemence, but her uncle could not forbear a parting shot. 'Tell you what,' he said, probably meaning it for a joke. 'In my opinion, the best way to settle the question would be to send over a shipload of whisky one day and a shipload of guns the next and they'd all get raving drunk and kill one another and save us the trouble.'

Robert stood up and his face was white with anger, but he only said a cold 'Good day' as he made for the door. His wife and sister ran to him and seized an arm each and his brother-in-law told him not to be a fool. 'It's only politics,' he said. 'You take things too

64

seriously. Come, sit down, and Edith'll tell the girl to bring in a cup of tea before you go on to Ann's.' But Robert walked out of the house and away down the street after saying over his shoulder to his wife, 'See you later.'

He had no sense of humour. None of them had at that moment. Laura's mother was all apologies. Her uncle, still angry, but a little ashamed, said he was sorry *for her*. Her aunt wiped her eyes on a pretty lace-edged handkerchief and Laura's needed wiping, for was not their long-looked-for day ruined if their lovely drive behind Polly had only led to this?

It was her mother, who did not pretend to be well-bred, yet always managed to do or say the right thing, who eased the situation by saying: 'Well, he'll have to come back presently to harness the horse and he'll be sorry enough by that time, I dare say, and I think I *will* have that cup of tea, if Bertha's got the kettle boiling. Just a cup to drink. Nothing more to eat, really. Then we must be getting on.'

VII

Kind Friends and Relations

After a decent interval, during which everybody tried to talk as though nothing had happened, the two children with their mother set out to follow their father to Aunt Ann's, Laura dragging behind a little, for the sun was hot and she was tired and not sure that she liked Candleford.

She soon cheered up; there was so much to see. Houses, houses all the way, not rows of houses, all alike, like peas in a pod, but big and little, tall and low, with old grey walls between with broken bottle-glass on the coping and fruit trees waving in gardens behind, and queer door-knockers and little shed-like porches, and people walking in their thin best shoes on the cobblestones with bunches of flowers, or prayerbooks, or beer jugs in their hands.

Once, at a turning, they caught a glimpse of a narrow lane of poor houses with ragged washing slung on lines between windows and children sitting on doorsteps. 'Is that a slum, Mother?' asked Laura, for she recognized some of the features described in the Sunday-school stories.

'Of course not,' said her mother crossly; then, after they had passed the turning: 'Don't speak so loud. Somebody might hear you and not like it. Folks who live in slums don't call them that. They're used to it and it seems all right to them. And why should you worry about things like that. You'd do better to mind your own business.'

Her own business! Wasn't it her business to be sorry for people who lived in slums and had no food or bed and a drunken father, or a landlord ready to turn them out in the snow. Hadn't her mother herself nearly cried when she read *Froggy's Little Brother* aloud to them? Laura could have cried then, in the middle of Candleford, at the thought of the time when Froggy took home the bloater as a treat and his poor little brother was too ill to eat any.

But they had come to a place where they could see green fields and a winding river with willows beside it. Facing them with its back to the fields was a row of shops, the last in the town on that side, and in the window of the shop they were approaching was nothing but one lady's top boot, beautifully polished and standing on an amber velvet cushion with an amber velvet curtain behind it. Above the window was a notice, unreadable to Laura then, but read by her many times afterwards, which said: 'Ladies' boots and shoes made to order. Best Materials. Perfect Workmanship. Fit Guaranteed. Ladies' Hunting Boots a Speciality.'

Their Uncle Tom had what was at that time called 'a snug little business'. It was a common thing then for people of all classes, excepting the very poorest, to have their footwear made to measure. In a large workshop across the yard at the back of the house and shop, workmen and apprentices scraped and hammered and sewed all day, making and mending. Uncle Tom's own workshop was a back room of the house, with a door opening out on to the yard, across which he came and went dozens of times a day to and from the main workshop. He made the hunting boots there and sewed the uppers of the more delicate makes, and there he fitted the customers, excepting the hunting ladies, who tried their boots on in the best parlour, Uncle Tom kneeling on the carpet before them like a courtier before a queen.

But all this Laura found out afterwards. On that first visit the front door flew open before they had reached it and they were surrounded by cousins and kissed and hugged and led to where Aunt Ann stood in the doorway.

Laura had never known any one like her Aunt Ann. The neighbours at home were kind in their rough way, but they were so bent on doing their best for themselves and those belonging to them that, excepting in times of illness or trouble, they had little feeling to spare for others. Her mother was kind and sensible and loved her children dearly, but she did not believe in showing too much tenderness towards them or in 'giving herself away' to the world at large. Aunt Ann gave herself away with every breath she drew. No one who heard her gentle voice or looked into her fine dark eyes could doubt her loving nature. Her husband laughed at what he called her 'softness' and said that customers calling in a great rage to complain that their shoes had not been delivered to time had stayed to tell the full story of their lives. For her own children she had sweet, pet names, and Edmund was soon her 'little lover' and Laura her 'Pussikins'. Except for her eyes and the dark, satiny hair which rippled in waves flat to her head, she was a plain-looking woman, pale and thin of face and of figure so flat that, with her hair parted in the middle and in the long, straight frocks she wore, she reminded Laura of Mrs Noah in the toy ark she had given Edmund at Christmas. That impression, a bony embrace, and a soft, warm kiss were all Laura had time for before she was borne on a stream of cousins straight through the house to an arbour in the garden where her father and uncle sat with a jug and glasses on a table between them and their pipes in their mouths. They were talking amiably together, although, only that morning, her father had spoken of her uncle as 'a snob' and her mother had protested, 'But he's not a common cobbler, Bob. He's a master man, and he makes more than he mends.'

If Laura's Uncle Tom was a snob by trade, there was nothing else snobbish about him, for he was one of the most liberal-minded men she was ever to know and one of the wisest. He was a Liberal in politics, too, and no doubt that accounted for her father's air of friendliness and ease. They were settling the Irish question, for the old familiar catchwords caught her ear, and it was rather an absent-minded uncle who stroked her hair and told the girls to take her to play in the orchard, but not to let the little boy go tumbling in the river, or their mother would have all those cakes she had been making left on her hands.

The orchard consisted of about a score of old apple and plum trees on a square of rough grass at the bottom of the garden, beyond which ran the small, sluggish stream, half choked with rushes and bordered with willows. Laura, who had felt so tired before, suddenly felt tired no more, but ran and shouted and played 'tig' with the others around the tree trunks. The apple blossom was nearly over and the petals were falling and they all tried to catch a petal or two because one of the cousins said that for every petal they caught they would have a happy month. Then there were small green gooseberries to crunch and forget-me-nots to pick. Laura filled her hands with these and carried them about until they drooped and had to be thrown into the river.

Gradually, she became able to distinguish between the new faces and to discover the name for each. There was Molly, the eldest, a motherly little person with a plump, soft figure, red-gold hair, and freckles on the bridge of her nose. Annie had reddish hair, too, but was smaller than Molly and had no freckles. Nellie was dark, quick in her movements, and said things that made people laugh. 'Sharp as a needle,' said Laura's father afterwards. Amy, the youngest girl, was Laura's own age. She had a red bow on her dark curls, but Laura did not need to look at the bow, except to admire it, because Amy was smaller than the others.

Johnny was the youngest of all, but by far the most important, for he was a boy, and a boy who came at the end of a long string of girls. Johnny must have anything he wanted, no matter to whom it belonged. If Johnny fell down, he must be picked up and comforted, and around Johnny, when he approached the river, red heads and dark heads drew to form a bodyguard. Rather a baby, thought Laura, although the same age as Edmund, who needed no attention at all, but went and stood on the bank and threw down twigs to float and called them ships; then ran, throwing up his heels like a young colt and lay on his back in the grass with his legs sticking up.

A shabby old flat-bottomed boat was moored beneath the bank, and when they were tired of their play, some one suggested that they should go and sit in it. 'But may we?' asked Laura, rather nervously, for it was the first boat she had seen outside a picture-book, and the water looked deep and wide to her, after the brook at home. But Edmund was more enterprising; he slid down the bank into the boat at once, crying: 'Come on! Hurry up! Our ship's just starting to Australia!' So, with the little boys holding an oar each and pretending to row, and the girls packed into the stern, well out

69

of the way of chance knocks with the oars, and the willow leaves silvery against the blue sky, and the air flavoured with mint and the raw dankness of water weeds, they set out on their imaginary voyage. And, all the time, there was that stout, strong rope holding the boat safely to shore. All the joys of adventure without its perils.

When discussing the family afterwards, Laura's mother said Molly was a little woman, 'a regular second mother to the younger ones', and her own mother must have trusted her, for the children were left to themselves the whole of that afternoon. Or it may have been that the father and uncle had so much to settle about Ireland and the mother and aunt were so busy indoors inspecting wardrobes and discussing family affairs.

The children, too, had plenty to discuss. 'Can you read?' 'When are you going to school?' 'What's Lark Rise like?' 'Only a few houses – all fields?' 'Where do you buy things if there are no shops?' 'Do you like Molly's hair? Most people hate red and they call her "ginger" at school; but Mr Collier, that's our Vicar, says it's lovely, and a customer told Mother that if she liked to have it cut off she could sell it for pounds and pounds. Some ladies would pay anything to have it to put on their own heads. Yes, didn't you know that some people wear false hair? Aunt Edith has a switch? I've seen it, hanging on her dressing-table in the morning; that's what makes her hair bunch out so at the back.' 'And your hair's nice, too, Laura,' said Molly generously, picking out Laura's best feature. 'I like the way it runs like water all down your back.'

'My mother can sit on her hair when it's down,' boasted Laura, and the cousins were impressed, for a great deal was thought of quantity in those days, of hair as of other things.

All the girls were going to school in the town as yet, but soon Molly and Nellie were to go to Miss Bussell's for a year each to be 'finished'. When, later, Laura asked her father if Johnny would go to Miss Bussell's, too, he laughed and said, 'Of course not. It's a girls' school. For the daughters of gentlemen, says the brass plate on the door, and that means for the daughters of a chimney sweep, if he can afford to pay.'

'Then where will Johnny go?' she persisted, and her father said,

'Eton, I s'pose,' which rather alarmed Laura because she thought he had said 'eaten'. She was relieved when he added, 'But I doubt if that'll be good enough. They'll have to build a special school on purpose for Johnny.'

What surprised Laura most as she listened to her cousins that afternoon was that they spoke of school as if they liked it. The hamlet children hated school. It was prison to them, and from the very beginning they counted the years until they would be able to leave. But Molly and Nellie and Amy said school was great fun. Annie did not like it so much.

'A-h-h! Who's bottom of her class!' laughed Nell.

But Molly said, 'Never mind her, Annie. She may be good at lessons, but she can't sew for nuts, and you're going to get the needlework prize with that baby's frock you're making. Ask her what Miss Pridham said when she examined her herring-boning.'

Then a voice from the upper garden called them in to tea. Just the kind of tea Laura liked, bread and butter and jam and a cake and some little cakes, a little more of everything than they had at home, but not the rich, bewildering abundance of the 'refreshments'.

She liked her cousins' house, too. It was old, with little flights of steps going up or down in unexpected places. Aunt Ann's parlour had a piano across one corner and a soft green carpet the colour of faded moss. The windows were wide open and there was a delicious scent of wallflowers and tea and cake and cobbler's wax. They had tea out of the silver teapot at the large round table in the parlour that day. Afterwards, they always had tea in the kitchen, much the nicest room in the house, with its two windows with window seats and brass warming pans and candlesticks and strips of red-and-blue striped matting on the stone floor.

That day, because they were having tea in the parlour, there was not room at the table for all, and Edmund and Johnny were seated at a side table with their backs to the wall, so that their respective mothers could keep an eye on them. But there was still so much talking going on among the elders that the little boys were forgotten until Johnny asked for more cake. When his mother handed him a slice he said it was too large, and, when halved, too small, and, finally, left the portion he had accepted in crumbs upon his plate, which shocked Edmund and Laura, who, at home, had to eat whatever was put upon their plates, and 'no leavings allowed'.

'Spoilt to death, regularly spoilt' was their mother's verdict when Johnny was spoken of afterwards, and perhaps at that time he was spoilt. He could scarcely escape spoiling, being the only and long-desired boy, coming after so many girls and then turning out to be the only delicate one of the family. He was young for his age and slow in developing; but there was fine stuff in Johnny. As a young man he was deeply religious, a non-smoker, a non-drinker and a non-card-player, and served the altar set up on many a battlefield during the 1914–18 War, and all this needed character in the atmosphere of Army life.

That Sunday afternoon Laura saw only a little boy with a pale, freckled face and thin fair hair. A spoilt child, of whom even his parents looked a little ashamed. But, in after years, she also saw Johnny as a sick soldier shut up in Kut, emaciated by illness and hunger and tormented by heat and flies; and that same soldier, once the adored little boy with his bodyguard of sisters, thrown out bodily after an exchange of sick prisoners with a last kick from his native jailor and a 'You can have this one for a makeweight. He's no good.' Or the same Johnny, lying for a whole summer on a long chair in the orchard, fed, every few minutes, as it seemed, with broth, or eggs beaten up in milk, out of teacups, until home and rest and his mother's nursing had strengthened him sufficient to pass his Board and be sent to the trenches in France. For, as we grow older, we see in memory not only our friends as they appeared to us as children, but also as they were to become in later years. The first sharp impression remains with us as a picture. Subsequent ones as a chain of episodes in a story, less positive, but more enlightening.

VIII

Sink or Swim

That journey to Candleford marked the end of Laura's childhood. Soon afterwards her schooldays began and she passed in one day from a protected home life to one where those who could had to fight for a place and maintain it by fighting.

The National School for the parish had been built in the mother village, a mile and a half from the hamlet. Only about a dozen children lived there and more than three times that number lived at Lark Rise; but, as the Church was there and the Rectory and the Manor House, it far outweighed the hamlet in importance. Up and down the long, straight road between the two places, the hamlet children travelled in bands. No straggling was allowed. An inclination to walk alone, or in twos or threes, was looked upon as an unpleasant eccentricity.

Most of the children were clean and at least moderately tidy when they left home, although garments might be too large or too small or much patched. 'Patch upon patch is better'n holes' was one of the hamlet mothers' maxims. The girls wore large white or coloured print pinafores over their ankle-length frocks, and their hair was worn scraped back from the brow and tied on the crown or plaited into a tight pigtail. Laura appeared on the first morning with her hair pushed back with an Alice in Wonderland comb under a pork-pie hat which had belonged to one of her cousins, but this style of headgear caused so much mirth that she begged that evening to be allowed to wear 'a real hat' and to have her hair plaited.

Her companions were strong, well-grown children between the ages of four and eleven. They ran and shouted and wrestled the whole way, or pushed each other over stoneheaps or into ditches, or stopped to climb into the hedges, or to make sorties into fields for turnips or blackberries, or to chase the sheep, if the shepherd was not handy.

Every one of the stoneheaps which dotted the grass margins at intervals for road-mending was somebody's castle. 'I'm the king of the castle. Get down, you dirty rascal!' was the cry of the first to reach and mount it, and he, or she, would hold it against all comers with kicks and blows. Loud cries of 'You're a liar!' 'You're another!' 'You daren't!' 'Yes, I dare, then!' 'Let's see you do it!' punctuated even their most peaceful games. There was no 'Sez you', or 'O.K., Chief', for the 'pictures' had not been invented, and the more civilizing wireless, with its Children's Hour, was still farther in the future. Even compulsory education was comparatively new. They were an undiluted native product.

There were times when they walked quietly, the elder ones talking like little old men and women, while the younger ones enlarged their knowledge of life by listening. Perhaps they would discuss the story of the snake, as thick as a man's thigh and yards long, which the shepherd had seen crossing that same road a few feet in front of him as he came home in the early morning from his lambing fold. Rather a puzzle to older people, that snake, for snakes are not usually abroad at lambing time, so it could not have been an English grass snake, magnified. Yet David was a sober, middle-aged man, unlikely to have invented the story. He must have seen something. Or perhaps the children would discuss their own and each other's chances of passing the next school examination. The shadow of a coming exam might account for their sedate behaviour. Or some one would relate how such-and-such a man had treated the foreman when he had 'tried to come it over him'; or the news would go round that So-and-So's mother was 'like to have another', much to the embarrassment of poor So-and-So. They talked about procreation and birth as soberly as little judges. 'What's the good of having a lot of brats you can't afford to feed,' one would say. 'When I'm married I shall only have one, or maybe two, in case one of 'em dies.'

The morning after a death in the hamlet would see them with

serious faces discussing the signs which were supposed to have
foretold it: the ticking of a death-watch spider, the unexplained
stopping of a clock, the falling of a picture from the wall, or the
beating of a bird's wings against the window. The formalities of the
death chamber fascinated them. They knew why and in what
manner the chin was tied up, of the plate of salt placed on the breast
of a corpse, and the new pennies used to weight down the eyelids.
This led naturally to ghost stories, and the smaller children on the
edge of the group would cease whispering among themselves and
press tightly in to the main throng for protection.

They did not mean to be cruel; but they were strong, hardy
children, without much imagination, and overflowing with energy
and high spirits which had to find an outlet. There was some bullying
and a great deal of boisterous teasing.

Once, on their way home from school, they overtook an old man.
So old that, as he dragged slowly along, his head was bent to the
level of the top of the stick which supported his footsteps. He was
a stranger, or the children would never have dared to mock, mob,
and insult him as they did. They knew that their parents and the
schoolmistress were unlikely to hear of it.

They did not actually strike him, but they hustled and pushed
him from behind, shouting: 'Old Benbow! Old Benbow!' Why
'Benbow', nobody knew, unless it was because his back was so bent.
At first he pretended to laugh at their attentions as a joke; but, soon,
growing tired of the pace they were forcing on him, he stood still
with them all about him, looked upward, shook his stick at them
and muttered a curse. At that they fell off, laughing, and ran.

It was a grey winter afternoon and, to Laura's eyes, the ancient,
solitary figure of the old man stood for a type of extreme desolation.
He had been young once, she thought, and strong; they would
not have dared to molest him then. Indeed, they were afraid of
able-bodied tramps and would run and hide from them. Now he
was old and poor and weak, and homeless, perhaps. Nobody cared
for him any more. What was the use of living at all if it was to
end like this, thought the little eight-year-old, and spent the rest of
the time going home in making up a story in which he figured as

a rich, handsome young man, until ruined by a bank failure (bank failures were frequent in juvenile fiction just then) and his lovely young wife died of smallpox and his only son was drowned at sea.

During her first year or two at school Laura came in for a good deal of teasing which she shared with two or three others whose looks, voices, parents or clothes did not please the majority. Not that there was anything objectionable about them, according to outside standards; it was only that they were a little different in some way from the accepted school pattern.

For instance, long frocks down to the ankles were still the hamlet wear for girls of all ages, while, in the outer world, the fashion had changed and little girls' frocks were worn extremely short. As Laura was fortunate, or unfortunate, enough to have the reversion of her cousins' wardrobes, she was put into short frocks prematurely. She was a little pleased and proud when she started off for school one morning in a cream cotton frock patterned with red dots that just touched her knees, especially as her mother, at the last moment, had found and ironed out a red hair-ribbon to go with it. But her pride had a fall when she was greeted with laughter and cries of 'Hamfrill!' and 'Longshanks!' and was told seriously by a girl who was usually friendly that she wondered that a nice woman like Laura's mother could allow her to go out like that.

She arrived home that evening a deplorable sight, for she had been tripped up and rolled in the dust and had cried so much that her face was streaked, and her mother – sympathetic for once, although she did not fail to remind her that 'sticks and stones break your bones, but calling names hurts nobody' – set to work upon the short frock and lengthened it sufficiently to reach to the calves of her legs. After which, if she stooped a little when any one looked directly at her, it passed muster.

There was one girl named Ethel Parker who at this time made Laura's life a misery to her. She professed friendship and would call for her every morning. 'So nice of Ethel,' Laura's mother said. Then, as soon as they were out of sight of the windows, she would either betray her to the gang – once by telling them Laura was wearing a red flannel petticoat – or force her to follow her through thorn hedges and over ploughed fields for some supposed short cut, or pull her hair, or wrench her arms, 'to try her strength', as she told her.

At the age of ten she was as tall and much stronger than most girls of fourteen. 'Our young Et's as strong as a young bullifant,' her father would say proudly. She was a fair-haired girl with a round, plump face and greenish eyes, the shape and almost the colour of a gooseberry. She had for cold weather a scarlet cloak, a survival of a fashion of some years before, and in this she must have looked a magnificent specimen of country childhood.

One of her pleasures was to make Laura gaze steadily at her. 'Now, see if you can stare me out,' she would say, and Laura would gaze slavishly into those hard, green eyes until her own fell before them. The penalty for flinching was a pinch.

As they grew older she used less physical violence, though she would still handle Laura pretty roughly under the pretence of play. She was what they called there 'an early-ripe' and, as she grew up, Laura's mother did not like her so much and told Laura to have as little to do with her as possible, adding, 'But don't offend her, mind. You can't afford to offend anybody in a place like this.' Then Ethel went away to a place in service and, a year or two later, Laura also left home and did not expect to see Ethel again.

But, fifteen years after, when living in Bournemouth, Laura, walking on the West Cliff one afternoon, a little out of her usual beat on some errand or other, saw coming towards her a large, fair young woman in a smartly-tailored suit with a toy dog under one arm and a pack of tradesmen's books in her hand. It was Ethel, by that time a cook-housekeeper, and out paying the household accounts and giving the family dog an airing.

She was delighted to see Laura, 'such an old friend and playmate'. What splendid times they had had and what scrapes they had got into together! Ah! There were no days like childhood's days and no friends like the old friends. Didn't Laura think so?

She was so enthusiastic and had so obviously forgotten every-thing unpleasant in their former association that Laura was almost persuaded that they really had been happy together, and was just going to ask Ethel to come to tea with her when the little dog under her arm began to fidget and she gave him a nip in the neck which quieted him. Laura knew that nip which made his eyes bulge, for she herself had felt it many times, and she knew that, beneath the smart clothes and improved manners, there was still the old Ethel. That was the last Laura ever saw of her; but she heard afterwards that she had married an ex-butler and opened a boarding-house. It is to be hoped that her guests were all people of strong character, for it is easy to imagine weaker ones quailing before those gooseberry eyes if they dared to make a request.

But the girls were not all like Ethel. Except when in contact with her and others of her kind, many were friendly, and Laura soon found out that her special mission in life was to listen to confidences. 'You are such a quiet little thing,' they would say, 'I know you won't tell anybody'; and afterwards: 'We've had such a nice talk,' although they had done every bit of the talking themselves, Laura's part in the conversation being limited to 'Yes' and 'No' and other sympathetic monosyllables.

Those girls who had sweethearts would talk about them by the hour. Did Laura not think Alfie good-looking? And he was strong, so strong that his father said he could carry a sack of potatoes that he himself could scarce lift, and his mother said he ate twice as much as his brothers; and, although you might not think it, he could be very agreeable when he chose. Only 'Saturday was a week' he had allowed the speaker to pick up and hold his catapult while he climbed down from a tree; 'that one in the corner of the meadow where the blacksmith's shop is, you know, Laura; there's nobody else in the school could climb it. That'll show you!' The remarkable thing about these love affairs was that the boys involved were usually unaware of them. A girl picked out a boy to be her sweetheart and sang his praises (to Laura, at least) and dreamed about him at night (or so she said) and treasured some worthless article which had belonged to him, and the utmost the boy did in return was to say 'Hullo!' when they met.

Sometimes it was difficult to decide upon a sweetheart. Then an ash leaf with nine leaflets had to be searched for, and, when found, placed in the seeker's bosom with the incantation:

> Here's an ash leaf with nine leaves on.
> Take it and press it to your heart
> And the first chap you meet'll be your sweetheart.
> If he's married let him pass by.
> If he's single, let him draw nigh,

and that usually did the trick, as there was but one side to that bargain.

Confidences about quarrels with other girls were even more frequent. What 'she said' and what 'I said', and how long it was since they had spoken to each other. But nearly every one had something to tell, if only what they had had for dinner on Sunday, or about the new frock they hoped to wear to church on Easter Day. This usually began as a red or blue velvet and ended by being 'that one of our young Nell's, turned and made shorter'. Laura would try to get in a word edgeways here, for she was fond of planning clothes. Her ideal frock at that time was a pale blue silk trimmed with white lace, and she always imagined herself riding in the station fly in it, as one of her aunts had ridden from the station when she came to them on a visit.

These confidences were all very well, if sometimes boring; but there were others which filled Laura's thoughts and weighed heavily upon her. Only one girl in the hamlet had a stepmother, and she was a model stepmother, according to hamlet standards, for she had no children of her own, and did not beat or starve her stepchildren. One of Laura's earliest memories was of the day on which Polly's own mother died. Polly, although a little older than Laura, could not remember so far back, and Laura must have been a very small child at the time. She was standing on the doorstep of her home on a misty morning when she heard a cock crow, very loudly and shrilly, and her mother, standing close behind her, said: 'At the house where that cock is crowing a little girl's mammy has died this morning.'

At the time of the school confidences, Polly was an unattractive-looking little girl, fat and pale, with scanty mouse-coloured hair, and heavy and clumsy in her movements. She breathed very heavily and had a way of getting very close to the person to whom she was talking. Laura almost hated herself for not liking her more; but she was really sorry for her. The stepmother, so fair-spoken to outsiders, was a tyrant indoors, and the stepchildren's lives were made miserable by her nagging. Every day – or every day when Polly could buttonhole Laura – there was some fresh story of persecution to be told and listened to. 'I know. I know,' Laura would say sympathetically, meaning that she understood, and Polly would retort, 'No, you don't know. Nobody could but them as has to put up with her,' and Laura would feel that her heart must break with the hopeless misery of it all. Her mother found her crying one day after one of Polly's confidences and demanded to be told the reason. 'Polly's not happy,' was all Laura could say, for she had sworn never to repeat what Polly had told her.

'Polly not happy? I dare say not,' said her mother dryly. 'None of us can be happy all the time; but your being unhappy as well doesn't seem to me to improve matters. It's no good, my girl, you've got to learn you can't take other people's troubles upon you. Do anything you can to help them, by all means, but their troubles are their own and they've got to bear them. You'll have troubles of your own before you have done, and perhaps by that time Polly'll be at the top of the tree of happiness. We all have our turn, and it only weakens us when our turn comes to have always been grieving about things we couldn't help. So, now, dry your eyes and come in and lay the table for tea and don't let me catch you crying again.' But Laura only thought her mother heartless and continued to grieve, until one day it suddenly struck her that it was only when she was alone with herself that Polly was miserable. When in company with the other girls she forgot her troubles and was as cheerful as her nature permitted, and, from that time, she took care to be less often alone with Polly.

No country child could be unhappy for long together. There were happy hours spent blackberrying, or picking bluebells or cowslips with a friend, or sitting in the long meadow grass making daisy or buttercup chains to be worn on the hair as a crown or as necklaces or girdles. When Laura was too old (according to others) to wear these herself, they could still be made for one of the younger children, who would stand, like a little statue, to be hung from head to foot with flowers, including anklets and earrings.

Sliding on the ice in winter was another joy. Not on the big slide, which was as smooth as glass and reached the whole length of the pond. That was for the strong, fighting spirits who could keep up the pace, and when tripped up themselves would be up in a moment and tripping up the tripper. Edmund was soon one of the leaders there, but Laura preferred some small private slide made by herself and a few friends and as near the bank as possible. How the cheeks glowed and the whole body tingled with warmth and excitement in the frosty air! And what fun it was to pretend that the arms stretched out for balance were wings and that the slider was a swallow!

Not such fun for Laura was the time when the ice gave way under her, and she found herself suddenly plunged into icy water. This was not the big pond, but a small, deep pool to which she and two other small girls had gone without asking permission at home. When they saw Laura drowning, as they thought, her companions ran off screaming for help, and Laura, left alone, was in danger of being sucked down under the ice; but she was near the bank and managed to grasp the branch of a bush and pull herself out before she realized her danger.

As she walked home across the fields her wet clothes froze upon her, and when she arrived dripping on the doorstep her mother was so cross that smacks, as well as hot bricks in bed, were administered to warm her. The wetting did her no harm. She did not even have a cold afterwards, although her mother had prophesied pneumonia. Another instance, she was told, of the wicked flourishing like a green bay-tree.

IX

Laura Looks On

Occasionally, during the school hours, something exciting would happen. Once a year the German band came and the children were marched out into the playground to listen. The bandsmen gave of their best at the school, for the mistress not only put a whole shilling in the collecting cap, but gave it with smiles and thanks and told the children to clap, and they clapped heartily, as they would have clapped anything which brought them out into the sunshine for a few minutes. When their shilling programme was finished, before playing 'God Save the Queen', the leader asked in his broken English if there was anything special 'the gracious lady' would like them to play. 'Home, Sweet Home' was the usual choice, but, one year, the mistress asked for 'When the Dewy Light was Fading', a Sankey and Moody hymn which had just then taken the neighbourhood by storm. When the musician shook his head and said, 'Sorry, not know,' his reputation went down considerably.

Once a grand funeral procession passed and the mistress told the children they might go out and watch it. It might be their last opportunity of seeing such a procession, she said, for times were changing and such deep, very deep mourning was becoming out of date.

It was the time of year when the buttercups were out on the road-margins and the hedges were white with may, and between them, at a snail's pace, came swaying a huge black hearse, draped with black velvet and surmounted at the four corners with bunches of black ostrich plumes. It was drawn by four coal-black horses with long, flowing tails, and driven and attended by undertaker's men with melancholy faces and with long black crape streamers floating from their top hats. Behind it came carriage after carriage of mourners, spaced out to make the procession as long as possible, and every carriage was drawn by its own black horse.

It passed slowly between the rows of open-mouthed, wondering children. There was plenty of time to look at it; but to Laura it did not seem real. Against the earth's spring loveliness the heavy black procession looked dream-like, like a great black shadow, Laura thought. And, in spite of the lavish display of mourning, it did not touch her as the country funerals did with their farm-wagon hearse and few poor, walking mourners crying into their handkerchiefs.

But she was so much impressed that she unintentionally started a rumour by saying that she thought such a grand funeral must be that of an earl. There was an aged nobleman living in the neighbourhood whose time must soon come in the course of Nature, and her 'an earl' became 'the earl' before it had been many times repeated. Fortunately for Laura, the schoolmistress heard this and corrected it by telling the children that it was the funeral of a farmer whose family had formerly lived in the parish and had a family burying place in the churchyard. Such a man would now be carried to his last resting-place in one of his own farm wagons and be followed by his near relatives in a couple of cars.

Then there was the day of the General Election, when little school work was done because the children could hear bands of voters passing beneath the school windows and shouts of 'Maclean! Maclean for Freedom! Maclean! Maclean! He be the boy for the farm labourer!' and they wished their schoolroom had been chosen for the polling station instead of the schoolroom in the next village. There was an uneasy feeling, too, because they knew their fathers were voting Liberal, and the mistress was wearing a bright blue rosette, the Conservative colour, which proclaimed her one with the Rectory and the Manor House, and against the villagers. The children were forbidden to wear the deep crimson which stood for the Liberal cause, but most of them carried a scrap of red in their pockets to wear going home and two or three of the more daring girls sported a red hair ribbon. The mistress was at liberty, too, to look out of the window, which they were not, and she made the most of this advantage, tiptoeing to open or shut it or arrange the blind whenever voices were heard. On one of these occasions she looked round at her scholars and said: 'Here, now, are two respectable men going quietly to vote, and as you may guess they are voting for law and order. It's a pity more in this parish are not like Mr Price and Mr Hickman' (the parson's factotum and the squire's gardener). At that, faces flared up and mouths grew sulky-looking, for the more intelligent took it as a reflection on their own fathers; but all such resentment was wiped out when she said at three o'clock: 'I think we had better dismiss now. You had better get home early, as it is Election Day.' Although it was a pity she added 'there may be drunken men about'.

But the most memorable day for Laura was that on which the Bishop came to consecrate an extension of the churchyard and walked round it in his big lawn sleeves, with a cross carried before him and a book in his hands, and the clergy of the district following. The schoolchildren, wearing their best clothes, were drawn up to watch. 'It makes a nice change from school,' somebody said, but to Laura the ceremony was but a prelude.

For some reason she had lingered after the other children had gone home, and the schoolmistress, who, after all, had not been invited to the Rectory to tea as she had hoped, took her round the church and told her all she knew of its history and architecture, then took her home to tea.

A small, two-roomed cottage adjoining the school was provided for the schoolmistress, and this the school managers had furnished in the manner they thought suitable for one of her degree. 'Very comfortable', they had stated in their advertisement; but to a new tenant it must have looked bare. The downstairs room had a deal table for meals, four cane-bottomed chairs of the type until recently seen in bedrooms, a white marble-topped sideboard stood for luxury and a wicker armchair by the hearth for comfort. The tiled floor was partly covered with brown matting.

But Miss Shepherd was 'artistic' and by the time Laura saw the room a transformation had taken place. A green art serge cloth with bobble fringe hid the nakedness of the deal centre table; the backs of the cane chairs were draped with white crocheted lace, tied with blue bows, and the wicker chair was cushioned and antimacassared. The walls were so crowded with pictures, photographs, Japanese fans, wool-work letter-racks, hanging pincushions, and other trophies of the present tenant's skill that, as the children used to say: 'You couldn't so much as stick a pin in.'

'Don't you think I've made it nice and cosy, dear?' said Miss Shepherd, after Laura had been shown and duly admired each specimen of her handiwork, and Laura agreed heartily, for it seemed to her the very height of elegance.

It was her first invitation to grown-up tea, with biscuits and jam – not spread on her bread for her, as at home, but spooned on to her plate by herself and spread exactly as she had seen her father spread his. After tea, Miss Shepherd played the harmonium and showed Laura her photographs and books, finally presenting her with one called *Ministering Children* and walking part of the way home with her. How thrilled Laura was when, at their parting, she said: 'Well, I think we have had quite a nice little time, after all, Laura.'

But, at the time of that tea-drinking, Laura must have been eleven or twelve, one of Miss Shepherd's 'big girls' and no longer an object of persecution. By that time the play was becoming less rough and bullying rarer, for the older children of her early schooldays had left school and none who came after were quite so belligerent. Civilization was beginning to tame them.

But, even in her earlier days, her life was easier after Edmund began school, for he was better-liked than she was; moreover, he could fight, and, unlike most of the other boys, he was not ashamed to be seen with his sister.

Often, on their way to school, Laura and he would take a field path which led part of the way by a brook backed by a pinewood where wood-pigeons cooed. By leaping the little stream, they could visit 'the graves'. These were two, side by side, in the deepest shade of the pines, and the headstones said: 'In Memory of Rufus' and 'In Memory of Bess'. They both knew very well that Rufus and Bess had been favourite hunters of a former owner of the estate; but they preferred to think of them as human beings – lovers, perhaps, who in life had been used to meet in that deep, mysterious gloom.

On other days they would scramble down the bank of the brook to pick watercress or forget-me-nots, or to build a dam, or to fish for minnows with their fingers. But, very often, they would pass along the bank without seeing anything, they would be so busy discussing some book they had read. They were voracious readers, although their books were few and not selected, but came to them by chance. There were the books from the school library, which, though better than nothing to read, made little impression upon them, for they were all of the goody-goody, Sunday-school prize type. But their father had a few books and others were lent to them, and amongst these were a few of the Waverley Novels. *The Bride of Lammermoor* was one of the first books Laura read with absorbed interest. She adored the Master of Ravenswood, his dark, haughty beauty, his flowing cloak and his sword, his ruined castle, set high on its crag by the sea, and his faithful servant Caleb and the amusing shifts he made to conceal his master's poverty. She read and re-read *The Bride* and dipped into it between whiles, until the heathery hills and moors of Scotland became as real to her as her flat native fields, and the lords and ladies and soldiers and witches and old retainers as familiar as the sober labouring people who were her actual neighbours.

At seven years old *The Bride* made such an impression upon her that she communicated her excitement to Edmund, himself as yet unable to read, and one night in their mother's bedroom they enacted the scene in the bridal chamber; Edmund insisting that he should be Lucy and Laura the bridegroom, although she had told him that a bridegroom was usually one of his own sex.

'Take up your bonny bridegroom!' he cried, so realistically that their mother came running upstairs thinking he was in pain. She found Laura crouching on the floor in her nightdress while Edmund stood over her with a dagger which looked very much like his father's two-foot rule. No wonder she said, 'Whatever will you two be up to next!' and took *The Bride of Lammermoor* away and hid it.

Then a neighbour who had bought a bundle of old books for a

few pence at a sale lent them *Old Saint Paul's*, and the outhouse door was soon chalked with a cross and the wheelbarrow trundled round the garden to the cry of 'Bring out your dead!'

Between the ages of seven and ten, Laura became such a confirmed reader that, when other books failed, she would read her father's dictionary, until this disappeared because her mother thought the small print was bad for her eyes. There was still the Bible, which could not be forbidden, and she spent many an hour over that, delighting in the Old Testament stories of the Pillar of Fire, and of Ruth and Esther and Samuel and David, and of Jonah and the whale, or learning by heart the parables in the New Testament to repeat at Sunday School. At one time she had a passion for the Psalms, not so much from religious fervour as from sheer delight in the language. She felt these ought to be read aloud, and, as she dare not read them aloud herself, lest she should be overheard, she would persuade Edmund or some other child to read them with her, verse and verse about.

Once, when Edmund was upstairs in bed with measles and her mother was out, she and another girl were having a fine time imitating the parson and clerk reading the Psalms in church, when Edmund, who could hear all that was going on downstairs, called out to ask whose Bible Alice was using. She was using his and when Edmund had his suspicions confirmed he was so enraged that he dashed downstairs in his nightshirt and chased Alice all down the garden to the gate. If his mother could have seen him out of doors with his spots, in his nightshirt, brandishing his Bible and threatening the retreating Alice, she would have been horrified, for measles patients were then told that they must not put so much as a hand out of bed or the spots would 'go inward' and the simple measles would turn to black measles, when they would probably die. But no one saw him and he returned to his bed, apparently not a ha-penny the worse for his airing.

A little later, Scott's poems came into their lives and Edmund would swing along the field path to school reciting 'The way was long, the night was cold', or stop to strike an attitude and declaim,

Come one, come all! this rock shall fly
From its stern base as soon as I,

or wave Laura on with 'Charge, Chester, charge! On, Stanley, on!' At that time their conversation when alone together was tinged with the language of their favourite romances. Sometimes Edmund would amuse his sister and himself by translating, when a battered old zinc bucket became 'ye antique pail', or a tree slightly damaged by the wind 'you lightning-blasted pine', while some good neighbour of theirs whom they could see working in the fields would have given Edmund what he would have called 'a darned good bommicking' if he had heard himself referred to as 'yon caitiff hind'.

Sometimes they tried their hand at writing a little verse themselves. Laura was guilty of a terrible moral story in rhyme about a good child who gave his birthday sixpence to a beggar, and Edmund wrote a poem about sliding on the ice with the refrain 'Slide, glide, glide, slide, over the slippery pond'. Laura liked that one and used to sing it. She also sang one of her own, beginning, 'The snowdrop comes in winter cold', which ran, with a stanza for every flower, through the seasons, and to which she added yet another stanza every time she saw or remembered a flower hitherto neglected. One day her mother asked her what that 'unked thing' she was trying to sing was about, and, in an unguarded moment, she brought out the scraps of paper on which it was written. She did not scold or even laugh at her folly; but Laura could feel that she was not pleased, and, later that evening, she lectured her soundly on her needlework. 'You can't *afford* to waste your time,' she said. 'Here you are, eleven years old, and just look at this seam!'

Laura looked; then turned away her face to hide her confusion. She did try to sew well; but, however hard she tried, her cotton would knot and her material pucker. She was supposed to be making stays for herself from narrow strips of calico left over from cutting out larger things, which, when finished with buttons and shoulder straps would make a lasting and comfortable garment. Laura always wore such stays; but not of her own making. If she had ever finished those she was working on, they would, by that time, have been too small to go round her. She saw them thirty years later in an old trunk of oddments with the strips puckered and the needle rusted into the material half-way up a seam, and remembered then the happy evening when her mother told her to put it aside and get on with her knitting.

By the eighteen-eighties the fine sewing of the beginning of the century was a lost art. Little children of six were no longer kept indoors to work samplers, whip cambric frills or stitch seams with stitches so tiny that a microscope was needed to examine them. Better uses had been found for young eyesight. But plain sewing was still looked upon as an important part of a girl's education, both at school and at home, for it was expected that for the rest of her life any ordinary girl would have at least to make her own underclothes. Ready-made clothes were beginning to appear in the shops, but those such as working people were able to buy were coarse, ugly, and of inferior quality. Calico stiffened with dressing which would all come out in the wash and leave the material like butter muslin, edging which looked like notched tape, and all put together with the proverbial hot needle and burning thread, tempted few people with self-respect to give up making their own underclothes.

If those who gave up outdoor pleasure and worked so busily in order that they might, as they said, know that all was good 'right to the skin' could have seen in a vision the lovely garments made of rayon and other materials of today, sold at less than their lengths of material cost, and all ready to step into, they would have thought the millennium was approaching.

But perhaps not. They might have thought the material too insubstantial to 'stand the wash' and so filmy it might show the figure through. Their taste ran to plenty of trimming; lace and insertion and feather-stitching on undergarments, flounces on frocks and an erection of ribbon and artificial flowers on hats. Laura's mother showed an almost revolutionary taste when she said: 'I don't care so much for an important-looking hat. I like something small and natty. But,' she would add apologetically to her listener, 'that may be because my face is small. I couldn't carry anything off like you can.'

The masterpiece of fashion during Laura's schooldays was what was known as the kilted frock. The skirt of this, over a pleated bottom part, had a kind of apron of the same material drawn up in folds round the hips and bunched out behind. It was a long time before any one in the hamlet possessed a kilted frock, but they were seen in church, and the girls in service came home for their holidays in them; then, as the fashion waned in the outer world, they began to arrive, either as gifts, or as copies of gifts made by some village dressmaker. And, with them, came the story that some great Parisian dress designer had invented the style after seeing a fisherwoman on the beach with her frock drawn up over her kilted petticoat, just in that manner. 'It's a corker to me how the de'il these 'oomen get to know such things,' said the men.

X

Summer Holiday

After that first visit to Candleford, it became the custom for Laura's parents to hire the innkeeper's horse and cart and drive there one Sunday in every summer; and, every summer, on the Sunday of the village feast, their Candleford aunt and uncle and cousins drove over to Lark Rise.

Then, one day when Laura was eleven and Edmund nine years old, their mother astonished them by asking if they thought they could walk over, just the two of them, by themselves. They had often walked to the market town and back, she reminded them. That was six miles and Candleford only eight. But did they think they could be trusted not to stray from the road ('No going into fields to pick flowers, Laura!') and would they be sure not to get into conversation with any strangers they might meet on the road, or be persuaded to follow them anywhere? It was their summer holiday from school and their Aunt Ann had written to ask them to spend a week or two with her and their cousins.

Could they manage the walk? What a question! Of course they could, and Edmund began to draw a map of the road to convince her. When could they go? Not before Saturday? What a long time to wait. But she said she must write to their aunt to tell her they were coming, then, perhaps, some of their cousins would walk out to meet them.

Saturday came at last and their mother waved to them from the gate and called out a last injunction not to forget the turnings, and, above all, not to have anything to do with strange men. She was evidently thinking of a recent kidnapping case which had been front-page news in the Sunday newspaper; but she need not have been afraid, no criminal was likely to be prowling about those unfrequented byways, and, had there been, the appearance of the two children did not suggest worthwhile victims.

'For comfort,' as their mother had said, they both wore soft, old cotton clothes: Laura a green smock which had seen better days but did not look too bad, well washed, and ironed, and Edmund an ex-Sunday white sailor suit, disqualified for better wear because the sleeves of the blouse and the legs of the knickers had been let down and the join showed. Both wore what were then known as Zulu hats, plaited of rushes and very wide brimmed, beneath which they must have looked like a couple of walking mushrooms. Most of the things necessary for their stay had been sent on by parcel post, but they still bulged with food packets, presents for the cousins, and coats for themselves in case of rain. Laura had narrowly escaped carrying an umbrella, for, as her mother persuasively said, if there was no rain she could use it as a sunshade; but, at the last minute, she had managed to put this down in a corner and 'forget' it.

They left home at seven o'clock on a lovely August morning. The mounting sun drew moisture in a mist from the stooks of corn in the partly stripped harvest fields. By the roadside all the coarse yellow flowers of later summer were out: goat's beard and lady's finger, tall thickets of ragwort and all the different hawkbits; the sun shone softly through mist; altogether, it was a golden morning.

A new field had been thrown open for gleaning and, for the first mile, they walked with some of their school-fellows and their mothers, all very jolly because word had gone round that young Bob Trevor had been on the horse-rake when the field was cleared and had taken good care to leave plenty of good ears behind for the gleaners. 'If the foreman should come nosing round, he's going to tell him that the ra-ake's got a bit out of order and won't clear the stubble proper. But that corner under the two hedges is for his mother. Nobody else is to leaze there.' One woman after another came up to Laura and asked in a whisper how her mother was keeping and if she found the hot weather trying. Laura had answered a good many such inquiries lately.

But the gleaners soon trooped through a gate and dispersed over the stubble, hurrying to stake out their claims. Then Edmund and Laura passed the school and entered on less familiar ground. They were out on their first independent adventure and their hearts thrilled to the new sense of freedom. Candleford waited so many miles ahead of them and it was nice to know that supper and a bed were assured to them there; but the pleasure they felt in the prospect of their holiday visit was nothing compared to the joy of the journey. On the whole, they would rather not have known where they were bound for. They would have liked to be genuine explorers, like Livingstone in Africa; but, as their destination had been decided for them, their exploring had to be confined to wayside wonders.

They found plenty of these, for it did not take much to delight them. A streak of clear water spouting from a pipe high up in the hedgerow bank was to them what a cataract might have been to more seasoned travellers; and the wagons they met, with names of strange farmers and farms painted across the front, were as exciting as hearing a strange language. A band of long-tailed tits, flitting from bush to bush, a cow or two looking at them over a wall, and the swallows strung out, twittering, along the telegraph wire, made cheerful and satisfying company. But, apart from these, it was not a lonely road, for men were working in the harvest fields on either side and they passed on the road wagons piled high with sheaves and saw other wagons go clattering, empty, back for other loads. Sometimes one of the wagoners would speak to them and Edmund would answer their 'An' where do 'ee s'pose you be off to, young shaver?' with 'We are going over to Candleford'; and they would both smile, as expected, when they were told, 'Keep puttin' one foot in front o' t'other an' you'll be there before dark.'

One exciting moment was when they passed through a village with a shop and went in boldly and bought a bottle of gingerade to wash down their sandwiches. It cost twopence and when they were told they must pay a halfpenny on the bottle they hesitated. But, remembering in time that they each had a whole shilling to spend, more than they had ever had at one time in their lives before, they paid up, like millionaires, and also invested in a stick of pink and white rock each, and, with one end wrapped in paper to keep

93

it from sticking to their fingers, went off down the road sucking.

But eight miles is a long walk for little feet in hot August weather, and the sun scorched their backs and the dust made their eyes smart and their feet ached and their tempers became uncertain. The tension between them reached breaking point when they met a herd of milking cows, ambling peacefully, but filling the narrow road, and Laura ran back and climbed over a gate, leaving Edmund to face them alone. Afterwards, he called her a coward, and she thought she would not speak to him for a long time. But, like most of her attempted sulks, it did not last, for she could not bear to be on bad terms with any one. Not from generosity of heart, for she often did not really forgive a real or imagined injury, but because she so much wanted to be liked that she would sometimes apologize when she knew the fault had not been hers.

Edmund was of a quite different nature. What he said he held to, like a rock. But then he did not say hasty, thoughtless things: what he said he meant and if any one was hurt by it, well, they were hurt. That did not change the truth, as he saw it. When he told Laura she was a coward he had not meant it unkindly; he was simply stating a fact and there was more of sorrow than of anger in his tone. And Laura only minded what he said so much because she was afraid it was true. If he had said she was stupid or greedy, she would only have laughed, because she knew she was neither.

Fortunately, soon after this, they saw what must have looked like a girls' school out for a walk advancing between the hedgerows to meet them. It was a relief party, consisting of the cousins and as many of their school friends as they could muster, with a large tin can of lemonade and some cakes in a basket. They all flopped down beside a little brook which crossed the road at that point and the girls fanned themselves with bunches of willow-herb and took off their shoes to search for stones, then dipped their toes in the water, and, before long, the whole party was paddling and splashing, which astonished Laura, who had always been told it would 'give anybody their death' to put the feet in cold water.

After that, it did not seem long before Candleford was reached and the travellers were being welcomed and made much of. 'They've walked! They've walked the whole way!' called their aunt to a friend who happened to be passing her door, and the friend turned and said, 'Regular young travellers, aren't they?' which made them again feel like the explorers they admired.

Then there was tea and a bath and bed, though not to sleep for a long time, for Laura had a bed in her two middle cousins' room and they talked a great deal. Talking in bed was a novelty to her, for it would not have been permitted at home. In her cousins' home there was more liberty. That night, once or twice one of their parents called upstairs telling them to be quiet and let poor little Laura get to sleep; but the talking went on, a little more quietly, until long after they heard the front door bolt shot and the window sashes in the lower rooms pushed up. What do little girls talk about when they are alone together? If we could remember that, we should understand the younger generation better than we do. All Laura could remember was that that particular conversation began with a cousin saying, 'Now, Laura, we want to know all about you,' and that in the course of it one of them asked her: 'Do you like boys?'

When she said, 'I like Edmund,' they laughed and she was told: 'I mean boys, not brothers.'

Laura thought at first they meant sweethearts and grew very hot and shy; but, no, she soon found they just simply meant boys to play with. She found afterwards that the boys they knew talked to them freely and let them join in their games, which surprised her, for the boys at home despised girls and were ashamed to be seen talking to one. The hamlet mothers encouraged this feeling. They taught their boys to look down upon girls as inferior beings; while a girl who showed any disposition to make friends of, or play games with, the boys was 'a tomboy' at best, or at worst 'a fast, forward young hussy'. Now she had come to a world where boys and girls mixed freely. Their mothers even gave parties to which both were invited; and the boys were told to give up things to the girls, not the girls to the boys – 'Ladies first, Willie!' How queer it sounded!

Candleford was but a small town and their cousins' home was on the outskirts. To children from a city theirs would have been a country holiday. To Laura it was both town and country and in that lay part of its charm. It was thrilling, after being used to walking miles to buy a reel of cotton or a packet of tea, to be able to dash out without a hat to fetch something from a shop for her aunt, and still more thrilling to spend whole sunny mornings gazing into shop windows with her cousins. There were marvellous things in the Candleford shops, such as the wax lady dressed in the height of fashion, with one of the new bustles, at the leading drapers; and the jeweller's window, sparkling with gold and silver and gems, and the toy shops and the sweet shops and, above all, the fishmonger's where a whole salmon reposed on a bed of green reeds with ice sprinkled over (ice in August! They would never believe it at home), and an aquarium with live goldfish swimming round and round stood near the desk where they took your money.

But it was just as pleasant to take out their tea in the fields (Laura's first experience of picnics), or to explore the thickets on the river banks, or to sit quietly in the boat and read when all the others were busy. Several times their uncle took them out for a row, right up the stream where it grew narrower and narrower and the banks lower and lower until they seemed to be floating on green fields. In one place they had to pass under a bridge so low that the children had to lie down in the boat and their uncle had to bow down his head between his knees until it almost touched the bottom. Laura did not like that bridge, she was always afraid that the boat would stick half-way through and they would never get out again. How lovely it was to glide through the farther arch and see the silvery leaves of the willows against the blue sky and the meadowsweet and willow-herb and forget-me-nots!

Her uncle exchanged 'Good morning's and words about the weather with the men working in the fields on the banks, but he did not often address them by name, for they were not close neighbours as the field workers were at home; and the farmers themselves, in this strange place, were not reigning kings, as they were at home, but mere men who lived by farming, for the farms around Candleford were much smaller.

On one of the first days of their holiday they went harvesting in the field of one of their uncle's customers, their share of the work, after they had dragged a few sheaves to the wagon, being to lie in the shade of the hedge and take care of the beer-cans and dinner baskets of the men, with occasional spells of hide-and-seek round the stooks, or rides for the lucky ones on the top of a piled-up wagon.

They had taken their own lunch, which they ate in the field, but at teatime they were called in by the farmer's wife to such a tea as Laura had never dreamed of. There were fried ham and eggs, cakes and scones and stewed plums and cream, jam and jelly and junket, and the table spread in a room as large as their whole house at home, with three windows with window seats in a row, and a cool, stone-flagged floor and a chimney corner as large as Laura's bedroom. No wonder Mr Partington liked that kitchen so much that his wife, as she told them, could never get him to set foot in the parlour. After he had gone back to the field, Mrs Partington showed them that room with its green carpet patterned with pink roses, its piano and easy chairs, and let them feel the plush of the upholstery to see how soft and deep it was, and admire the picture of the faithful dog keeping watch on its master's grave, and the big photograph album which played a little tune when you pressed it.

Then Nellie had to play something on the piano, for no friendly call was then considered complete without some music. People said Nellie played well, but of this Laura was no judge, although she much admired the nimble way in which her hands darted over the keyboard.

Afterwards they straggled home through the dusk with a corn-crake whirring and cockchafers and moths hitting their faces, and saw the lights of the town coming out, one by one, like golden flowers, as they entered. There was no scolding for being late. There was stewed fruit on the kitchen table and a rice pudding in the oven, of which those who felt hungry partook, and glasses of milk all round. And, even then, they did not have to go to bed, but went out to help water the garden, and their uncle told them to take off their shoes and stockings, then turned the hose upon them. Wet frocks and petticoats and knicker legs resulted; but their aunt only told them to bundle them all up and put them into the cupboard under the attic stairs. Mrs Lovegrove was coming to fetch the washing on Monday. It was a surprising household.

Every few days, when they were out in the town, they would call at Aunt Edith's, at their Aunt Ann's request, 'in case she should be hurt, if neglected'. Uncle James would be about his business; the girls were away on a visit, and even Aunt Edith herself would often be out shopping, or at a sewing party, or gone to the dressmaker's. Then Bertha would take them straight through to her kitchen and give them cups of milk in order to detain them, for although so silent as to be thought simple in the presence of the elders, with the children alone she became talkative. What did Molly, or Nellie, think of so-and-so, which had happened in the town? What was Mr Snellgrave up to when he fell down those stone steps? 'Was he a bit tight, think you?' She had heard, though it wouldn't do for Master to know, that he called at the 'Crown' for his glass every night, and him a sidesman and all. Still, it might, as Molly suggested, have been that the steps were slippery after the shower. But you couldn't help thinking! And had they heard that her Ladyship up at Bartons was getting up one of these new fancy bazaars? It was to be held in the picture gallery and anybody could go in who cared to pay sixpence; but she expected they'd have to buy something – crocheted shawls and hand-painted plates and pincushions and hair-tidies – all given by the gentry to sell for the heathens. 'No, not the Candleford heathens. Don't be cheeky, young Nell. The heathen blacks, who all run naked in foreign parts, like they have the collection for in church on missionary Sundays. I expect the Mis'is will go and your mother and some of you. They say there's tea going to be sold at sixpence a cup. Robbery, I call it! but there's them as'd pay as much as a pound only to get their noses inside Bartons, let alone sitting down and drinking tea with the nobs.'

Bertha was not above school gossip, either. She took great interest in children's squabbles, children's tea parties and children's holidays. 'There, did you ever! – I wonder, now, at that!' she would ejaculate on hearing the most commonplace tittle-tattle and remember it and comment on it long after the squabble had been made up and the party forgotten by all but her.

In spite of her spreading figure and greying hair, there was something childlike about Bertha. She was excessively submissive before her employers, but, alone with the children, with whom she apparently felt on a level footing, she was boisterous and slangy. Then she was so pleased with little things and so easily persuaded, that she actually seemed unable to make up her mind on any subject until given a lead. She had an impulsive way, too, of telling something, then begging that it might never be repeated. 'I've been and gone and let that blasted old cat out of the bag again,' she would say, 'but I know I can trust you. You won't tell nobody.'

She let a very big cat out of the bag to Laura a year or two later. Laura had gone to the house alone, found her Aunt Edith out, and was sipping the usual cup of milk in the kitchen and paying for it with small talk, when a very pretty young girl came to the back door with a parcel from Aunt Edith's dressmaker and was introduced to her as 'our young Elsie'. Elsie could not stay to sit down, but she kissed Bertha affectionately and Bertha waved to her from the doorway as she crossed the yard.

'What a pretty girl!' exclaimed Laura. 'She looks like a robin with those rosy cheeks and all that soft brown hair.'

Bertha looked pleased. 'Do you see any likeness?' she asked, drawing up her figure and brushing her hair from her forehead.

Laura could not; but, as it seemed to be expected, she ventured: 'Well, perhaps the colour of her cheeks . . .'

'What relation would you take her for?'

'Niece?' suggested Laura.

'Nearer than that. You'll never guess. But I'll tell you if you'll swear finger's wet, finger dry, never to tell a soul.'

Not particularly interested as yet, but to please her, Laura wetted her finger, dried it on her handkerchief, drew her hand across her throat and swore the required oath; but Bertha, her cheeks redder than ever, only sighed and looked foolish. 'I'm making a fool of myself again, I know,' she said at last, 'but I said I'd tell you, and, now you have sworn, I must. Our young Elsie's my own child.

I gave birth to her myself. I'm her mother, only she never calls me that. She calls our Mum at home Mother and me Bertha, as if I was her sister. Nobody here knows, only the Mis'is, and I expect the Master and your Aunt Ann, though they've never either of them mentioned it, even with their eyes, and I know I oughtn't to be telling you at your age, but you are such a quiet little thing, and you saying she was pretty and all, I felt I must claim her.'

Then she told the whole story, how she had, as she said, made a fool of herself with a soldier when she was thirty and ought to have known better at that age, and how Elsie had been born in the Workhouse and how Aunt Edith, then about to be married, had helped her to send the baby home to her mother and advanced money from her future wages to get herself clothes, and taken her into her new home as a maid.

Laura felt honoured, but also burdened, by such a confidence; until one day, when they were speaking of Bertha, Molly said, 'Has she told you about Elsie?' Laura must have looked confused, for her cousin smiled and went on, 'I see she has. She's told me and Nellie, too, at different times. Poor old Bertha, she's so proud of "our young Elsie" she must tell somebody or burst.'

Except for these calls and a formal tea-drinking at Aunt Edith's once or twice in every holiday, the children spent their time at Aunt Ann's.

The class to which she and her husband belonged is now extinct. Had Uncle Tom lived in these days, he would probably have been manager of a branch of one of the chain stores, handling machine-made footwear he had not seen until it came from the factory. Earning a good salary, perhaps, but subject to several intermediary 'superiors' between himself and the head of the firm and without personal responsibility for, or pride in, the goods he handled: a craftsman turned into a salesman. But his day was still that of the small business man who might work by his own methods at his own rate for his own hours and, afterwards, enjoy the fruits of his labour and skill, both in the way of satisfaction in having turned out good things, and in that of such comforts for himself and his family as his profits could afford. What these profits should be, his customers decided; if he could please them they came again and again and sent others and that meant success. Except his own conscience as a craftsman, he had nothing but his customers to consider. Twice a year he went to Northampton to buy leather, choosing his own and knowing what he chose was good because, owing no merchant a long bill, he was not tied to any and could choose where he would. It was a simple life and one which many might well envy in these days of competition and carking care.

His was a half-way house between the gorgeous establishment of their other uncle and their own humble home. There was nothing pretentious. Far from it, for pretentiousness was the one unpardonable sin in such homes. But there was solid comfort and not too close a scrutiny of every shilling spent. When Aunt Ann wrote out her grocery list, she did not have to cut out and cut out items, as their mother had to do, and they never once heard from her the familiar 'No, no. It can't be done' they were so used to hearing at home.

There were other advantages. Water had not to be drawn up from a well, but came from a bright brass tap over the kitchen sink, and the sink was another novelty; at home the slops were put in a pail which, when full, had to be carried out of doors and emptied on the garden. And the w.c. – a real w.c. – although not actually indoors, was quite near, in a corner of the yard, and reached by a covered pathway. Then there was no big washing-day to fill the house with the steam of suds and leave behind a mass of wet clothes to be dried indoors in bad weather, for a woman came every Monday morning and carried the week's washing away, and when she brought it back clean at the end of the week she stayed to scrub out the stone-floored kitchen and passage, sluice down the courtyard and clean the windows.

The water was pumped up to a cistern in the roof every morning by the boy who swept out the shop and carried the customers' parcels and, in between, was supposed to be learning the trade, although, as Uncle Tom told him, he would never make a good snob, his backside was too round – meaning that he would never sit still long enough. Benny was a merry, good-natured lad who performed all kinds of antics and made ridiculous jokes, which the children relished greatly. Sometimes, as a great favour, he would let them take a turn with the pump-handle. But he soon seized it again, for he could not stand still a moment. He would jump on the pump-handle and ride it; or stand on his head, or turn somersaults, or swarm up a water-pipe to an outhouse roof and sit, grimacing like a monkey, on the ridge tiles. He never walked, but progressed by hopping and skipping or galloping like a horse, and all this out of sheer lightheartedness.

Poor Benny! he was then fourteen and had all the play of a lifetime to crowd into a very few years. He was an orphan who had been brought up in the Workhouse, where, as he told the children, ''em 'udn't let you speak or laugh or move hardly,' and the recent release of his high spirits seemed to have intoxicated him.

He did not live in the house, but had been put out to board with an elderly couple, and Aunt Ann was so afraid that they would forget he was a growing boy that she seldom saw him without giving him food. A cup of milk and a doorstep of bread and jam rewarded him for the pumping every morning and he never returned from an errand for her but she put an apple or a bun or a slice of something into his hand. No baking was complete without a turnover of the oddments being made for Benny.

All, excepting the poorest, kept house extravagantly in those days of low prices. Food had to be of the best quality and not only sufficient, but 'a-plenty', as they expressed their abundance. 'Do try to eat this last little morsel. You can surely find room for that and it's a pity to waste it,' they would say to each other at table and some one or other would make room for the superfluous plateful; or, if no human accommodation could be found, there were the dogs and cats or a poorer neighbour at hand.

Many of the great eaters grew very stout in later life; but this caused them no uneasiness; they regarded their expanding girth as proper to middle age. Thin people were not admired. However cheerful and energetic they might appear, they were suspected of 'fretting away their fat' and warned that they were fast becoming 'walking miseries'.

Although Laura's Aunt Ann happened to be exceptionally thin and her uncle was no more than comfortable of figure, the usual abundance existed in their home. There were large, local-grown joints of beef or lamb, roasted in front of the fire to preserve the juices; an abundance of milk and butter and eggs, and cakes and pies made at a huge baking once or twice a week. People used to say then, 'I'd think no more of doing it than of cracking an egg,' little dreaming, dear innocents, that eggs one day would be sixpence each. A penny each for eggs round about Christmas was then thought an exorbitant price. For her big sponge cake, a speciality of hers, Aunt Ann would crack half a dozen. The mixture had to be beaten for half an hour and the children were allowed to take turns at her new patent egg-beater with its handle and revolving wheels. Another wonder of her kitchen was the long fish kettle which stood under the dresser. That explained what was meant by 'a pretty kettle of fish'. Laura had always imagined live fish swimming round and round in a tea kettle.

Before they had been at Candleford a week a letter came from their father to say they had a new little sister, and Laura felt so relieved at this news that she wanted to stand on her head, like Benny. Although no hint had been dropped by her elders, she had known what was about to happen. Edmund had known, too, for several times when they had been alone together he had said anxiously, 'I hope our mother's all right.' Now she was all right and they could fully enjoy their holiday.

Ordinary mothers of that day would put themselves to any inconvenience and employ any subterfuge to prevent their children suspecting the advent of a new arrival. The hint of a stork's probable visit or the addition of a clause to a child's prayers asking God to send them a new little brother or sister were devices of a few advanced young parents in more educated circles; but even the most daring of these never thought of telling a child straightforwardly what to expect. Even girls of fifteen were supposed to be deaf and blind at such times and if they accidentally let drop a remark which showed they were aware of the situation they were thought disagreeably 'knowing'. Laura's schoolmistress during Bible reading one day became embarrassed over the Annunciation. She had mentioned the period of nine months; then, with blushing cheeks and downcast eyes, said hastily: 'I think nine months is the time a mother has to pray to God to give her a baby before her prayer is answered.' Nobody smiled or spoke, but hard, cold eyes looked at her from the front row where her elder pupils sat, eyes which said as plainly as words, 'You must think we're a lot of softies.'

After the baby's arrival, if the younger children of the family asked where it had come from, they were told from under a gooseberry bush, or that the midwife had brought it in her basket, or the doctor in his black bag. Laura's mother was more sensible than most parents. When asked the question by her children when very small she replied: 'Wait until you get older. You're too young to understand, and I'm sure I'm not clever enough to tell you.' Which perhaps was better than confusing their young minds with textbook talk about pollen and hazel catkins and bird's eggs, and certainly better than a conversation between a mother and child on the subject which figured in a recent novel. It ran something like this:

'Mother, where did Auntie Ruth get her baby?'

'Uncle Ralph and she made it.'

'Will they make some more?'

'I don't think so. Not for some time at any rate. You see, it is a very messy business and frightfully expensive.'

That would not have passed with a generation which knew its Catechism and could repeat firmly: 'God made me and all the world.'

What impressed Laura most about Candleford, on that first holiday there, was that, every day, there was something new to see or do or find out and new people to see and talk to and new places to visit, and this gave a colour and richness to life to which she was unaccustomed. At home, things went on day after day much in the same manner; the same people, all of whom she knew, did the same things at the same time from week-end to week-end. There you knew that, while you were having your breakfast, you would hear Mrs Massey clattering by on her pattens to the well, and that Mrs

Watts would have her washing out first on the line and Mrs Broadway second every Monday morning, and that the fish-hawker would come on Monday and the coalman on Friday and the baker three times a week, and that no one else was likely to come nearer than the turning into the main road.

Of course, there were the changes of the seasons. It was delightful on some sunny morning in February, one of those days which older people called 'weather-breeders', to see the hazel catkins plumping out against the blue sky and to smell the first breath of spring in the air. Delightful, too, when spring was nearer, to search the hedgerows for violets, and to see the cowslips and bluebells again and the may, and the fields turning green, then golden. But all these delights you expected; they could not fail, for had not God Himself said that seedtime and harvest, summer and winter, should endure as long as the world lasted? That was His promise when He painted the first rainbow and set it in the sky as a sign.

But at Candleford these things did not seem so important to Laura as they did at home. You had to be alone to enjoy them properly; while games and fun and pretty clothes and delicious food demanded company. For about a week of her visit Laura wished she had been born at Candleford; that she was Aunt Ann's child and had lots of nice things and was never scolded. Then, as the week or two for which they had been invited drew out to nearly a month, she began to long for her home; to wonder how her garden was looking and what the new baby was like and if her mother had missed her.

The last day of their holiday was wet and one of the cousins suggested they should go and play in the attic, so they went up the bare, steep stairs, Laura and Ann and Amy and the two little boys, while the two elder girls were having a lesson in pastry-making. The attic, Laura found, was a storehouse of old, discarded things, much like the collection Mrs Herring had stored in the clothes closet at home. But these things did not belong to a landlady; they were family possessions with which the children might do as they liked. They spent the morning dressing up for charades, an amusement Laura had not heard of before, but now found entrancing. Dressed in apron and shawl, the point of the latter trailing on the ground behind her, she gave her best imitation of Queenie, an old neighbour at home who began most of her speeches with 'Lawks-a-mussy!' Then, draped in an old lace curtain for veil, with a feather duster for bouquet, she became a bride. Less realistically, no doubt, for she had never seen a bride in conventional attire – the girls at home wore their new Sunday frock to be married – but her cousins said she did it well and she became very pleased with herself and full of ideas for illustrating words which she kept to herself for future use at home, for she felt too much of a novice to venture suggestions.

All the morning, first one cousin then another had been running down to the kitchen to ask for suggestions for the charades. They always came back munching, or wiping crumbs from their mouths, and once or twice they brought tit-bits for the whole party. At last they all disappeared, Edmund included, and Laura was left alone in her bridal finery, which she took the opportunity of examining in a tall, cracked mirror which leaned against one wall. But her own reflection did not hold her more than a moment, for she saw in the glass a recess she had not noticed before packed with books. Books on shelves, books in piles on the floor, and still other books in heaps, higgledy-piggledy, as though they had been turned out of sacks. Which they had, no doubt, for she was told afterwards that the collection was the unsaleable remains of a library from one of the large houses in the district. Her uncle, who was known to be a great reader, had been at the sale of furniture and been told that he might have what books were left if he cared to cart them away. A few of the more presentable bindings had already been taken downstairs; but the bulk of the collection still awaited the time when he should not be too busy to look through them.

That attic was very quiet for the next quarter of an hour, for Laura, still in her bridal veil, was down on her knees on the bare boards, as happy and busy as a young foal in a field of green corn.

There were volumes of old sermons which she passed over quickly; a natural history of the world which might have detained her had there not been so many other vistas to explore; histories and grammars and lexicons and 'keepsakes' with coloured pictures of beautiful languishing ladies bending over graves beneath weeping willows, or standing before mirrors dressed for balls, with the caption 'Will he come tonight?' There were old novels, too, and poetry. The difficulty was to know what to look at first.

When they missed her downstairs and came to call her to dinner she was deep in Richardson's *Pamela, or Virtue Rewarded*, and it was afterwards a standing joke against her that she had jumped and looked dazed when Amy hissed into her ear, 'Do you like apple dumplings?'

'Laura's a bookworm, a bookworm, a bookworm!' she sang to her sisters with the air of having made an astonishing discovery, and Laura wondered if a bookworm might not be something unpleasant until she added: 'A bookworm, like Father.'

She had brought the first volume of *Pamela* down with them to illustrate Laura's bookworminess and now asked her mother if Laura might not have it to keep. After glancing through it, her mother looked doubtful, for she gathered that it was a love story, though not, perhaps, the full extent of its unsuitability for a reader of such tender age. But Uncle Tom, coming in just then to his dinner and hearing the whole story, said 'Let her keep it. No book's too old for anybody who is able to enjoy it, and none too young, either, for that matter. Let her read what she likes, and when she's tired of reading to herself she can come to my shop and read to me while I work.'

'Poor Laura! You're in for it!' laughed mischievous Nell. 'Once you start reading to Dad, he'll never let you go. You'll have to sit in his smelly old shop and read his dry old books for ever.'

'Now! Now! The less you say about that the better, my girl. Who was it came to read to me and made such a hash of it that I never asked her to come again?'

'Me', and 'Me', and 'Me', cried the girls simultaneously, and their father laughed and said: 'You see, Laura, what a lot of dunces they are. Give them one of their mother's magazines, with fashion pictures and directions for making silk purses out of sows' ears and pretty little tales that end in wedding bells, and they'll lap it up like a cat lapping cream; but offer them something to read that needs a bit of biting on and they're soon tired, or too hot, or too cold, or they can't stand the smell of cobbler's wax, or think they hear somebody knocking at the front door and have to go to open it. Molly started reading *The Pilgrim's Progress* to me over a year ago – her own choice, because she liked the pictures – and got the poor fellow as far as the Slough of Despond. Then she had to take an afternoon off to get a new frock fitted. Then there was something else, and something else, and poor Christian is still bogged up in the slough for all she knows or cares. But we won't have *The Pilgrim's Progress* when you read to me, Laura. That is a shade dull for some young people. I've read it a good many times and hope to read it a good many more before I wear my eyesight out getting a living for these ungrateful young besoms. A grand old book, *The Pilgrim's Progress*! But I've something here you'll like better. *Cranford*. Ever heard of it, Laura? No, I thought not. Well, you've got a treat in store.'

They sampled *Cranford* that afternoon, and how Laura loved dear Miss Matty! Her uncle was pleased with her reading, but not too pleased to correct her faults.

Seated on the end of the bench on which he worked, with both arms extended as he drew the waxed thread through the leather, his eyes beaming mildly through his spectacles, he would say: 'Not too fast now, Laura, and not *too* much expression. Don't overdo things. These were genteel old bodies, very prim and proper, who would not have raised their voices much if they'd heard the last trump sounding.' Or, more gently, in a matter-of-fact tone, as if, although it did not matter much how words were pronounced as long as one knew their meaning, it might still be just as well to conform to usage: 'I think that word is pronounced so-and-so, Laura,' and Laura would repeat the syllables after him until she had got it more or less correctly. Having read so much to herself and being a rapid reader, she knew the meanings of hundreds of words which she had never even attempted to pronounce until she came to read aloud to her uncle. Though he must have been sorely tempted to do so, he never once smiled, even at her most grotesque efforts. Years later in conversation he pronounced magician 'magicun' and added, 'as Laura once called one of that kidney', and they both laughed heartily at the not altogether inapt rendering.

XI

Uncle Tom's Queer Fish

The readings were continued the next summer, when Laura again spent her summer holidays with her cousins, and afterwards, when Candleford became for several years her second home. Every afternoon when her cousins could be persuaded to go out or do what they wanted to do without her, she would tap at the door of her uncle's workshop and hear the familiar challenge, 'Who goes there?' and reply, 'Bookworms, Limited,' and, receiving the password, go in and sit by the open window looking out on the garden and river and read while her uncle worked.

Their reading was often interrupted, for customers came and went, or sat down to chat in a special chair with a cushion, 'the customer's chair'. Many sat in that chair who were not there on business, for her uncle had many friends who liked to look in when passing, especially on days when there was something of special interest in the newspaper. 'Just wanted to know what you thought of it,' they would say, and Laura noticed that whatever opinion he had given them was adopted so thoroughly that it was often advanced as their own before they left.

In the evening his workshop became a kind of a club for the young working-men of the neighbourhood, who would sit around on upturned boxes, smoking and talking or playing draughts or dominoes. Uncle Tom said he liked to see their young faces round him, and it kept them out of the 'pub'. Their arrival was the signal for Laura to take up her book and depart; but, when a day caller arrived, she would sit still in her corner, reading, or trying to solve that maddening puzzle of the day, 'Getting the teeth in the nigger's mouth'. The mouth belonged to a face enclosed in a circular glass case and the teeth were small metal balls which were easier to scatter than to get into place. One, two, or three, might with infinite patience be coaxed to rest between the thick lips, but the next gentle jerk, intended to place a fourth, would send them all rolling around beneath the glass again. Laura never got more than three in. But perhaps she did not persevere sufficiently; it was much more interesting to listen.

Uncle Tom had many friends. Some of these, as might have been expected, were fellow tradesmen of the town who looked in upon him to pass the time of day, as they said, or to discuss the news or some business complication. Others were poor people who came to ask his advice on some point, or to ask him to sign a paper, or to bring him something out of their gardens, or merely to rest and talk a few minutes. Few of these ever spoke to Laura, beyond a casual greeting, but she came to know them and could remember their faces and voices when those of others who had been more to her had become dim. But it was those Nellie described as 'Dad's queer fish' that she liked best of all. There was Miss Connie, who wore a thick tweed golf cape and spiked boots, even in August. 'Let Laura take your cape and sit down and cool off a bit,' Uncle Tom would say to her when the sun was raging and there was scarcely a breath of air in the shop, even with both windows wide open. 'No. No, thanks, Tom. Don't touch it, please, Laura. I wear it to keep the heat from the spine. The spine should always be protected.'

Miss Constance kept nineteen cats in the big house where she lived alone, for she could not trust servants; she thought they would always be spying upon her. Sometimes a kitten would thrust its head between the edges of her cape as she talked. 'Now, don't you worry, Miss Constance,' Uncle Tom would be saying. 'You'll get your money all right come quarter day. Some lawyers are rogues, we know, but not Mr Steerforth. And nobody can harm you for keeping your cats, for your house is your own. And don't take any notice of what you heard Mrs Harmer say; though, if you'll excuse me for saying it, Miss Constance, I do think you've got quite enough of them. I wouldn't save any more kittens, if I were you; and, if you can't bear a maid about the place, why not get some decent, respectable woman to come in once or twice a week and clean up a bit? Somebody who likes cats. No. She wouldn't poison them, nor steal your things. Bless you, there are very few thieves about compared to the number of honest people in the world. And don't you worry, Miss Constance, or you'll lose all your pussies. Worry killed the cat, you know,' and at that often-repeated joke Miss Constance would smile and the smile would transform the poor, half-mad recluse she was fast becoming to something resembling the bright, happy girl who had danced all night and ridden to hounds in the days when Uncle Tom had first fitted her for her country shoes.

But even Miss Constance was not quite so strange as the big fat man who wore the dark inverness cloak and soft black felt hat. He was a poet, Laura was told, and that was why he dressed like that and wore his hair so long. He came every market day, having walked from a village called Isledon, six or seven miles away, and, after puffing and blowing and mopping his brow, he would draw out a paper from his breast pocket and say, 'I must read you this, Tom,' and Uncle Tom would say, 'So you've been at it again. Oh, you poets!' To her great disappointment, although she listened intently, Laura could never grasp exactly what his poems were about. There were eagles in most of them, but not the kind of eagles she had read of, which circled over mountains and carried off lambs and babies; these eagles of his were eagles one moment and Pride or Hate the next; and if there were flowers in his poems he had always chosen the ugliest, such as nightshade or rue. But it all sounded very learned and grand, read in his rich, sonorous voice, and she had the comfort of knowing that, if she could not make much sense of it, her uncle could not either, for she heard him say many times: 'You know I'm no judge of poetry. If it were prose now . . . But it's certainly got a fine roll and swell to it. That I do know.'

After the reading, they would settle down to talk about flowers and birds and what was going on in the fields, for the poet loved all these, although he did not write about them. Or sometimes he would talk of his home and children and praise his wife for allowing him to come away into the country alone for a whole summer to write. 'Shows she believes in you as a poet,' Uncle Tom said once, and the poet drew himself up from his chair and said, 'She does and she'll be justified, though perhaps not in my lifetime. Posterity will judge.'

'Fine words! Fine words!' said Uncle Tom after he had gone. 'But I doubt it. I doubt.'

Less odd, and therefore less interesting to Laura, though dearer to her Uncle Tom's heart, was the young doctor with the keen, eager face and grey eyes set deep under heavy dark brows. From what she heard then, she thought, looking back in after years, that he was trying to work up a practice and finding it heavy going. He certainly had a good deal of spare time.

'It's a rotten shame,' he would begin, as he burst into the work-shop and turned up the tails of his frock coat to keep them from contact with the customers' chair. 'It's a rotten shame' was the beginning of most of his conversations. It was a rotten shame that cottage roofs should leak, that children living on farms should not know the taste of fresh milk, that wells should be in use of which the water was contaminated, or that families should have to sleep eight in a room.

Uncle Tom was just as sorry about it all as he was; but he was not so angry; though Laura did once hear him say that something they were talking about was damnable. 'You take things too hard,' Laura once heard him say. 'You fret, and it's no good fretting. You can only do what you can, and God knows you're doing your full share. Things'll be better in time. You mark my words, they will. They're better already: you should have seen Spittals' Alley when I was a boy!' And when the young man had taken down his top hat from the shelf which was kept covered with clean paper for its reception, and jammed it down on his head and gone out, still declaring that it was a rotten shame, her uncle said, perhaps to her, perhaps to himself: 'That young fellow-me-lad's going to make a big stir in the world, or else he's going to build up a fat practice, marry and settle down, and I don't know which to wish for him.'

It was the young doctor who named Laura 'the mouse'. 'Hullo, Mouse!' he would say if he happened to notice her. That seldom happened, for he had no eye for plain little girls with books on their knees, unless they were ill or hungry. When one of her pretty cousins burst in at the door, her healthy high spirits stirring the air like a breeze, his face lit up, for she was the type of what he believed all children would be, if they could be properly fed and cared for.

Excepting the doctor, none of those known as Uncle Tom's 'queer fish' seemed to have any work to do or business to attend to, and, excepting Miss Connie, none of them were Candleford people. Some were regular visitors to farmhouses where boarders were taken; others were staying for the fishing at village inns, or had their own homes in one of the surrounding villages. Uncle Tom's chief friend among them, a Mr Mostyn, took a furnished cottage outside the town every summer. How they had first become acquainted, Laura never heard, but by the time of her regular visits to Candleford he was a frequent visitor.

Even in his holiday attire of shabby Norfolk suit and sandals, no one could have mistaken Mr Mostyn for anything but what was then spoken of openly and unashamedly as 'a gentleman'. Uncle Tom was a country shoemaker. He had black thumbs, worked in an apron, and carried the odours of leather and wax about with him; but he was the least class-conscious man on earth, and Mr Mostyn appeared equally so, though breeding may have had something to do with that on his side. While Uncle Tom sewed, they would talk by the hour; about books, about historical characters, new discoveries in science or exploration, with many a tit-bit of local gossip thrown in and many a laugh, especially when Tom told some story in dialect. Or they would sit silent if that suited either of them better than talking. Mr Mostyn would take a book out of his pocket and read; or, in the midst of a conversation, Tom would say, 'Not another word, now, till I've got this seam joined up. I've cut the toecap a bit short, I find.' In fact, they were friends.

But one year, when Laura arrived, she found things had changed between them. Mr Mostyn still called at the workshop once or twice a week and they still talked – talked more than ever before, indeed – but upon a new subject. Mr Mostyn was thinking of changing his creed, 'going over to Rome', Uncle Tom called it, and, surprisingly, for a man who believed in perfect freedom of thought, he did not approve of this step.

It was strange to see how earnest he was about it; for, although he went to church every Sunday, he had never appeared to take any special interest in religion. Mr Mostyn, probably, had hitherto taken less. Laura had often heard him say that he preferred a good long tramp on a Sunday to church-going. Now, something had stirred him; he had been reading Catholic doctrine for months and was on the brink of being received into the Catholic Church.

Uncle Tom must have read, too, at some time, for he appeared to know the authors his friend quoted. 'That's Newman,' he said once. 'Methinks his lordship doth protest too much'; and, at another time, 'He can write like an angel, I grant you, but it's all spellbinding.'

Mr Mostyn gritted his teeth. 'Tom, Tom,' he said, 'your other name is Didymus!'

'Now, look here,' said Tom. 'We've got to get to grips with this. If you want everything thought out for you and to be told what to think and do, give your conscience to some priest to keep; go over to Rome. You couldn't do better. It'll be a rest for you, I don't deny, for you've had your problems, as many and hard as most men; but if, as a reasoning being, you prefer to accept full responsibility for your own soul, you are going the wrong road – you are, indeed!' Then Mr Mostyn said something about peace, and Tom retorted, 'Peace in exchange for liberty!' and Laura heard, or understood, no more.

'Another good man gone over to the old enchantress,' he said, as the door closed behind his friend; and Laura, who was by that time nearly fourteen, asked, 'Do you think it wrong to be a Catholic, Uncle?'

It was some time before he answered. She thought he had forgotten her presence and had been talking to himself. But, after he had polished his spectacles and taken up his work, he answered, 'Wrong? No, not for those born to it or suited to it. I've known some good Catholics in my time; some the religion suited like the glove the hand. It was a good thing for them, but it won't be for him. He's been over a year thinking it out and studying books about it, and if you have to spend a year worrying and arguing yourself into a thing, that thing's against your nature. If he'd been cut out for a Catholic, he'd have just sunk down into it months ago, as easy as falling into a feather bed, and not had to lash and worry himself and read his eyes out. But, for all that, I've been a fool to try to influence him, trying to influence him against being influenced. Never try to influence anybody, Laura. It's a mistake. Other people's lives are their own and they've got to live them, and often when we think they are doing wrong they are doing right – right for them, although it might not be right for us. Come, get that book and see how Lucy Snowe's getting on with her Frenchman, and I'll stick to my last, as every good shoemaker should do, and not go airing my opinions again – until the next time.'

Once a commercial traveller called at the workshop to have a stitch or two put in the shoes he was wearing. He was a stranger to Laura; but not to her uncle, for one of the first questions he asked was, 'How is your wife?'

'Lazier and more contrary than ever,' was the unconventional reply.

Uncle Tom looked grave, but he said nothing. The visitor needed no encouragement, however; he was soon launched on a long story of how he had that very morning taken up his wife's breakfast to her in bed – so many rashers, so many eggs, and toast and marmalade. Breakfast in bed for any one who was not ill was a novel idea to Laura; but her Uncle Tom seemed to look upon it as a slight attention any good husband might pay his wife, for he only said, 'That was very kind of you.'

'And what did I get for my kindness?' almost shouted the husband. 'No thanks, you'll bet! but only black looks and an order to be home on time tonight for once in my life. Home on time! Me, who, as she ought to know by this time, might be held up for hours on end by a customer. Of all the spiteful, contrary cats . . .'

Uncle Tom looked distressed. 'Hush! Hush! my lad,' he interposed. 'Don't say things you'll be sorry for after. How long have you been married? Two years, and no child yet? Well, you wait till you've been married ten before you begin talking like that, and by that time, if you do as you should yourself, it's ten to one you'll not need to. Some women simply can't understand what business is unless they see for themselves. Why not take her out on the round a time or two in that smart little outfit of yours with the high-stepper. The firm's done you well this time, I see, in that respect. A nice bit of horseflesh, if I'm any judge! If you do that, she'll see for herself, and the outing will do her good. It's dull for a young woman, shut up by herself in the house all day, and when, towards night, her man's supper's drying up in the oven through waiting, it gets on her nerves and maybe her welcome's not all a husband might wish, after a trying day and not too many orders in his notebook. And when you get a bit nettled yourself, bite on it, bite on it, my boy; don't go opening your mouth to fill other folks's. They won't think any better of you if you do. Truth of the matter is, most married folks have their little upsets, especially for the first year or two; but they manage to pretend that all is well and that everything in the garden of matrimony looks lovely, and, in ninety-nine cases out of a hundred, before they know where they are, all *is* well, or as well as can be expected in this imperfect world.'

During this long speech the young man had broken in several times with such ejaculations as 'That's all very well' or 'Not half ', but he was spared the necessity for any formal comment upon what was almost a lecture by a sound of scuffling and 'Whoa-a-s!' and 'Come up nows!' in the street, which caused him to cram on the shoe which Tom had been attending to and run. But, a few minutes later, very flushed and hot-looking, he came to the open window and said: 'That mare of mine's got the spirit of a racehorse. A moment more and she'd been off! Got an idea I'll bring my wife next week; she could hold the reins and read her book while I was inside anywhere, and the outing might do her good. So long, Mr Whitbread. I must go or she'll kick the cart to bits.'

Laura never knew if the mare kicked the cart to bits; or if the young couple's own little applecart of happiness was overturned or steadied; but she can still see the young husband's face flushed and distorted with indignation beneath the white straw 'boater', moored so modishly to his button-hole by a black cord, and her Uncle Tom's pale and grizzled and serious, looking up at him through his spectacles as he said: 'Bite on it, my boy. Bite on it.'

XII

Candleford Green

On one of her visits to Candleford, Laura herself found a friend, and one whose influence was to shape the whole outward course of her life.

An old friend of her mother's named Dorcas Lane kept the Post Office at Candleford Green, and one year, when she heard that Laura was staying so near her, she asked her and her cousins to go over to tea. Only Molly would go; the others said it was too hot for walking, that Miss Lane was faddy and old-fashioned, and that there was no one to talk to at Candleford Green and nothing to see. So Laura, Edmund, and Molly went.

Candleford Green was at that time a separate village. In a few years it was to become part of Candleford. Already the rows of villas were stretching out towards it; but as yet the green with its spreading oak with the white-painted seats, its roofed-in well with the chained bucket, its church spire soaring out of trees, and its clusters of old cottages, was untouched by change.

Miss Lane's house was a long, low white one, with the Post Office at one end and a blacksmith's forge at the other. On the turf of the green in front of the door was a circular iron platform with a hole in the middle which was used for putting on tyres to wagon and cart wheels, for she was wheelwright as well as blacksmith and postmistress. She did not work in the forge herself; she dressed in silks of which the colours were brighter than those usually worn then by women of her age and had tiny white hands which she seldom soiled. Hers was the brain of the business.

To go to see Cousin Dorcas, as they had been told to call her, was an exciting event to Laura and Edmund, for they hoped to be shown her famous telegraph machine. There had been some talk about it at home when their parents heard it had been installed, and their mother, who had seen one, described it as a sort of clock face, but with letters instead of figures, 'and when you turn the handle,' she said, 'the hand goes round and you can spell out words on it, and that sends the hand round on the clock face at the other Post Office where it's for, and they just write it down, pop it into an envelope, and send it where it's addressed.'

'And then they know somebody's going to die,' put in Edmund.

'After they've paid three and sixpence,' said their father, rather bitterly, for an agitation was being worked up in the hamlet against having to pay that crushing sum for the delivery of a telegram. 'For Hire of Man and Horse, 3s. 6d.' was written upon the envelope and that sum had to be found and paid before the man on the horse would part with the telegram. But about that time, the innkeeper, tired of having to lend three and sixpence with little prospect of getting it back, every time the news arrived that some neighbour's father or mother or sister or aunt was 'sinking fast' or had 'passed peacefully away this morning', had, in collaboration with a few neighbours of whom the children's father was one, written a formal and much-thought-out protest to the Postmaster General, which resulted in men coming with long chains to measure the whole length of the road between the hamlet and the Post Office in the market town. The distance was found to be a few feet under, instead of over, the three-miles limit of the free delivery of telegrams. This made quite an interesting little story for Laura to tell Cousin Dorcas. 'And to think of those poor things having paid that sum! As much as a man could earn in a day and a half's hard work,' was her comment, and there was something in the way she said it that made Laura feel that, although, as her cousins said, Miss Lane might be peculiar, it was a nice kind of peculiarity.

Laura liked her looks, too. She was then about fifty, a little, birdlike woman in her kingfisher silk dress, with snapping black eyes, a longish nose, and black hair plaited into a crown on the top of her head.

The famous telegraph instrument stood on a little table under

her parlour window. There was a small model office for the trans-
action of ordinary postal business, but 'the telegraph' was too secret
and sacred to be exposed there. When not in use, the dial with its
brass studs, one for every letter of the alphabet, was kept under a
velvet cover of her own devising, resembling a tea-cosy. She
removed this to show the children the instrument and even allowed
Laura to spell out her own name on the brass studs – without
putting the switch over, of course, or, as she said, Head Office would
wonder what they were up to.

Edmund preferred the forge to the telegraph office, and Molly
the garden where Zillah, the maid, was picking greengages bursting
with ripeness. Laura liked all these; but, best of all, she liked Cousin
Dorcas herself. She said such quick, clever things and seemed to
know what one was thinking before a word was spoken. She showed
Laura her house, from attic to cellar, and what a house it was! Her
parents had lived in it, and her grandparents, and it was her delight
to keep all the old family possessions just as she had inherited them.
Other people might scrap their solid old furniture and replace it
with plush-covered suites and what-nots and painted milking-stools
and Japanese fans; but Dorcas had the taste to prefer good old oak
and mahogany and brass, and the strength of mind to dare to be
thought old-fashioned. So the grandfather's clock in the front kitchen
still struck the hours as it had done on the day of the Battle of
Waterloo. The huge, heavy oak table at the head of which she
carved for the workmen and maid, sitting in higher or lower seats
according to degree, was older still. There was a legend that it had
been made in the kitchen by the then village carpenter and was too
large to remove without taking it to pieces. The bedrooms still had
their original four-posters, one of them with blue-and-white check
curtains, the yarn of which had been spun by her grandmother on
the spinning wheel lately rescued from the attic, repaired and placed
with the telegraph instrument in the parlour. On the dresser shelves
were pewter plates and dishes, with a few pieces of old willow-
pattern 'to liven them up', as she said; and in the chimney corner,
where Laura sat looking up into the square of blue sky through the
black furry walls, a flint and tinder box, used for striking lights

before matches were in common use, stood on one ledge, and on another stood a deep brass vessel with a long point for sticking down into the embers to heat beer. There were brass candlesticks on the mantelpiece, and, flanking it, a pair of brass warming-pans hung on the wall. These were no longer in use, nor was the sandbox for drying wet ink instead of using blotting-paper, nor the nest of wooden chopping bowls, nor the big brewing copper in the back kitchen, but they were piously preserved in their old places, and, with them, as many of the old customs as could be made to fit in with modern requirements.

The grandfather's clock was kept exactly half an hour fast, as it had always been, and, by its time, the household rose at six, break-fasted at seven and dined at noon; while mails were despatched and telegrams timed by the new Post Office clock, which showed correct Greenwich time, received by wire at ten o'clock every morning.

Miss Lane's mind kept time with both clocks. Although she loved the past and tried to preserve its spirit as well as its relics, in other ways she was in advance of her own day. She read a good deal, not poetry, or pure literature – she had not the right kind of mind for that – but she took in *The Times* and kept herself well-informed of what was going on in the world, especially in the way of invention and scientific discovery. Probably she was the only person on or around the Green who had heard the name of Darwin. Others of her interests were international relationships and what is now called big business. She had shares in railways and the local Canal Com-pany, which was daring for a woman in her position, and there was an affair called the Iceland Moss Litter Company for news of which watch had to be kept when, later, Laura was reading the newspaper aloud to her.

Had she lived later she must have made her mark in the world, for she had the quick, unerring grasp of a situation, the imagination to foresee and the force to carry through, which meant certain success. But there were few openings for women in those days, especially for those born in small country villages, and she had to be content to rule over her own small establishment. She had been thought queer and rather improper when, her father having died and left his business to her, his only child, instead of selling out and retiring to live in ladylike leisure at Leamington Spa or Weston-super-Mare, as her friends had expected, she had simply substituted her own name for his on the billheads and carried on the business.

'And why not?' she asked. 'I had kept the books and written the letters for years, and Matthew is an excellent foreman. My father himself had not put foot inside the shop for ten months before he died.'

Her neighbours could have given her many reasons why not, the chief one being that a woman blacksmith had never been known in those parts before. A draper's or grocer's shop, or even a public-house, might be inherited and carried on by a woman; but a blacksmith's was a man's business, and they thought Miss Lane unwomanly to call herself one. Miss Lane did not mind being thought unwomanly. She did not mind at all what her neighbours thought of her, and that alone set her apart from most women of her day.

She had consented to house the Post Office temporarily in the first place, because it was a convenience badly needed on and around the Green, and no one else could be found willing to undertake the responsibility. But the work soon proved to be a pleasure to her. There was something about the strict working to a time-table, the idea of being a link in a great national organization and having some small measure of public authority which appealed to her businesslike mind. She liked having an inside knowledge of her neighbours' affairs too – there is no denying that – and to have people coming in and out, some of them strangers and interesting. As she ran the office, she had many of the pleasures of a hostess without the bother and expense of entertaining.

She had arranged her Post Office with its shining counter, brass scales, and stamps, postal orders, and multiplicity of official forms neatly pigeonholed, in what had been a broad passage which ran through the house from the front door to the garden. The door which led from this into the front kitchen, where meals were taken, marked the boundary between the new world and the old. In after days, when Laura had read a little history, it gave her endless pleasure to notice the sudden transition from one world to the other.

It was still the custom in that trade for unmarried workmen to live-in with the families of their employers; and, at mealtimes, when the indoor contingent was already seated, sounds of pumping and sluicing water over hands and faces would come from the paved courtyard outside. Then 'the men', as they were always called, would appear, rolling their leather aprons up around their waists as they tiptoed to their places at table.

The foreman, Matthew, was a bow-legged, weak-eyed little man with sandy whiskers, as unlike as possible the popular picture of a village blacksmith. But he was a trustworthy foreman, a clever smith, and, in farriery, was said to approach genius. The three shoeing-smiths who worked under him were brawny fellows, all young, and all of them bashful indoors; although, by repute, 'regular sparks' when out in the village, dressed in their Sunday suits. Indoors they spoke in a husky whisper; but in the shop, on the days when they were all three working there together, their voices could be heard in the house, above the roaring of the bellows and the cling-clang of the anvil as they intoned their remarks and requests to each other, or sang as an anthem some work-a-day sentence, such as 'Bil-h-l-l, pass me o-o-over that sm-m-a-ll spanner.' When Matthew was out of the way, they would stand at the shop door for 'a breather', as they called it, and exchange pleasantries with passers-by. One had recently got into trouble with Cousin Dorcas for shouting 'Whoa, Emma!' after a girl; but no one who only saw him at table would have thought him capable of it.

There, the journeymen's place was definitely below the salt. At the head of the long, solid oak table sat 'the mistress' with an immense dish of meat before her, carving knife in hand. Then came a reserved space, sometimes occupied by visitors, but more often blank table-cloth; then Matthew's chair, and, after that, another, smaller blank space, just sufficient to mark the difference in degree between a foreman and ordinary workmen. Beyond that, the three young men sat in a row at the end of the table, facing the mistress. Zillah, the maid, had a little round table to herself by the wall.

Unless important visitors were present, she joined freely in the conversation; but the three young men seldom opened their mouths excepting to shovel in food. If, by chance, they had something they thought of sufficient interest to impart, they always addressed their remarks to Miss Lane, and prefixed them by 'Ma-am'. 'Ma-am, have you heard that Squire Bashford's sold his Black Beauty?' or 'Ma-am, I've heard say that two ricks've bin burnt down at Wheeler's. A tramp sleeping under set 'em afire, they think.' But, usually, the only sound at their end of the table was that of the scraping of plates, or of a grunt of protest if one of them nudged another too suddenly. They had special cups and saucers, very large and thick, and they drank their beer out of horns, instead of glasses or mugs. There were certain small delicacies on the table which were never offered them and which they took obvious pains not to appear to notice. When they had finished their always excellent meal, one of them said 'Pardon, Ma-am,' and they all tiptoed out. Then Zillah brought in the tea-tray and Matthew stayed for a cup before he, too, withdrew. At tea-time they all had tea to drink, but Miss Lane said this was an innovation of her own. In her father's time the family had tea alone, it was their one private meal, and the men had what was called 'afternoon bavour', which consisted of bread and cheese and beer, at three o'clock.

As a child, Laura thought the young men were poorly treated and was inclined to pity them; but, afterwards, she found they were under an age-old discipline, supposed, in some mysterious way, to fit them for becoming in their turn master-men. Under this system, such and such an article of food was not suitable for the men; the men must have something substantial – boiled beef and dumplings, or a thick cut off a gammon, or a joint of beef. When they came in to go to bed on a cold night, they could be offered hot spiced beer, but not elderberry wine. They must not be encouraged to talk and you must never discuss family affairs in their presence, or they might become familiar; in short, they must be kept in their place, because they were 'the men'.

Until that time, or a few years earlier in more advanced districts, these distinctions had suited the men as well as they had done the employers. Their huge meals and their beds in a row in the large attic were part of their wages, and as long as it was excellent food and the beds were good feather beds with plenty of blankets, they had all they expected or wished for indoors. More would have embarrassed them. They had their own lives outside.

When a journeyman was about to marry, it was the rule for him to leave and find a shop where the workers lived out. There was no difficulty about this, especially in towns, where the living-out system was extending, and a good workman was always sure of employment. The young men who still lived in did so from choice; they said they got better food than in lodgings, better beds, and had not to walk to their work at six o'clock in the morning.

Miss Lane's own father had come to the Green as a journeyman, wearing a new leather apron and with a basket of tools slung over his shoulder. He had walked from Northampton, not on account of poverty, for his father was a master-man with a good smithy in a village near that town; but because it was the custom at that time that, after apprenticeship, a young smith should travel the country and work in various shops to gain experience. That was why they were called 'journeymen', Miss Lane said, because they journeyed about.

But her own father journeyed no farther, for his first employer had a daughter, Miss Lane's mother. She was an only child and the business was a flourishing one, and, although the new journeyman was the son of another master-smith, her parents had objected to the match.

According to her daughter's story, the first intimation they had of the budding attachment was when her mother found her Katie darning the journeyman's socks. She snatched them out of her hand and threw them into the fire and her father told her he would rather see her in her coffin than married to a mere journeyman. After all they had done for her, she should marry at least a farmer. However, they must have become reconciled to the match, for the young couple married and lived with the parents until the father died and they inherited the house and business. There was a painting of them in their wedding clothes in the parlour; the bridegroom in lavender trousers and white kid gloves (How did he manage to squeeze his smith's horny and ingrained hands into them?), and the dear little bride in lavender silk with a white lace fichu and a white poke bonnet encircled with green leaves.

When she was old enough, little Dorcas had been sent to school as a weekly boarder and the school must have been even more old-fashioned than her home. The girls, she said, addressed each other as Miss So-and-So, even during playtime, and spent some time every day lying flat on the bare board floor of their bedroom to improve their figures. Their punishments were carefully calculated to fit their crimes. The one she remembered best and often laughed about later was for pride or conceit, which was standing in a corner of the schoolroom and repeating 'Keep down, proud stomach', patting the said organ meanwhile. They learned to write a beautifully clear hand, to 'cast up accounts', and to do fine needlework, which was considered a sufficient education for a tradesman's daughter eighty or ninety years ago.

Once, when she was turning out a drawer to show Laura some treasure, she came upon a white silk stocking, which she held up for inspection. 'How do you like my darning?' she asked; but it was not until Laura had drawn the stocking over her own hand to examine it more closely that she saw that the heel and the instep and part of the toe were literally made of darns. The silk of the original fabric had been matched exactly and the work had been exquisitely done in a stitch which resembled knitting.

'It must have taken you ages,' was the natural comment.

'It took me a whole winter. Time thrown away, for I never wore it. My mother turned it out from somewhere and gave it me to darn at such times as the men were indoors. It was not thought proper then to do ordinary sewing before men, except men's shirts, of course; never our own underclothes, or anything of that kind; and as to reading, that would have been thought a waste of time; and one must not sit idle, that would have been setting a bad example; but cutting holes in a stocking foot and darning them up again was considered industrious. Be glad you weren't born in those days.'

Although she could darn so beautifully, she no longer darned her own stockings. She left them to Zillah, whose darns could easily be seen across the room. Probably she felt she had done enough darning for one lifetime.

Belonging to the establishment was a light spring-cart and a bright chestnut mare named Peggy and, three times a week, Matthew and two of the shoeing smiths drove off with strings of horseshoes and boxes of tools to visit the hunting stables. Sometimes the remaining smith was out also and the forge was left, cold and silent and dark, save for the long streamers of daylight which filtered through the cracks in the shutters. Then Laura would steal in through the garden door and inhale the astringent scents of iron and oil and ashes and hoof-parings; and pull the bellows handle and see the dull embers turn red; and lift the big sledge hammer to feel its weight and made the smaller ones tinkle on the anvil. Another lovely sound belonging to the forge was often heard at night when the household was in bed, for then the carrier, returning from market, would fling down on the green in front of the shop the long bars of iron for making horseshoes. *Cling-cling, cling*, it would go, like a peal of bells. Then the carrier would chirrup to his tired horse and the heavy wheels would move on.

All kinds of horses came to the forge to be shod: heavy cart-horses, standing quiet and patient; the baker's and grocer's and butcher's van horses; poor old screws belonging to gipsies or fish-hawkers; and an occasional hunter, either belonging to some visitor to the neighbourhood or one from a local stable which had cast a shoe and could not wait until the regular visiting day. There were a few donkeys in the neighbourhood, and they, too, had to be shod; but always by the youngest shoeing smith, for it would have been beneath the dignity of his seniors to become the butt for the wit of the passers-by. 'He-haw! He-haw!' they would shout. 'Somebody tell me now, which is top-most, man or beast, for danged if I can see any difference betwixt 'em?'

Most of the horses were very patient; but a few would plunge and kick and rear when approached. These Matthew himself shod and, under his skilful handling, they would quiet down immediately. He had only to put his hand on the mane and whisper a few words in the ear. It was probably the hand and voice which soothed them; but it was generally believed that he whispered some charm which had power over them, and he rather encouraged this idea by saying when questioned: 'I only speaks to 'em in their own language.'

The local horses were all known to the men and addressed by them by name. Even the half-yearly bills were made out: 'To So-and-So, Esq. For shoeing Violet, or Poppet, or Whitefoot, or The Grey Lady.' 'All round', or 'fore', or 'hind', as the case might demand. Strings of horseshoes, made in quiet intervals, hung upon the shop walls, apparently ready to put on; but there was usually some little alteration to be made on the anvil while the horse waited. 'No two horses' feet are exactly alike,' Matthew told Laura. 'They have their little plagues and peculiarities, like you and me do.' And the parting words from man to beast were often: 'There, old girl, that's better. You'll be able to run ten miles without stopping with them shoes on your feet.'

Other items which figured in the bills were making hinges for doors, flaps for drains, gates and railings and tools and household requirements. On one occasion a bill was sent out for 'Pair of Park Gates to your own design, £20', and Matthew said it should have been fifty, for he had worked on them for months, staying in the shop hours after the outer door was closed, and rising early to fit in another hour or two before the ordinary work of the day began. But it was a labour of love, and, after they were hung, he had his reward when he, who so seldom went out for pleasure, dressed on a Sunday and took a walk that way in order to admire and enjoy his own handicraft.

So the days went on, and, secure in the knowledge of their own importance in the existing scheme of things, the blacksmiths boasted: 'Come what may, a good smith'll never want for a job, for whatever may come of this new cast-iron muck in other ways, the horses'll always have to be shod, and they can't do that in a foundry!'

Yet, as iron will bend to different uses, so will the workers in iron. Twenty years later the younger of that generation of smiths were painting above their shop doors, 'Motor Repairs a Speciality', and, greatly daring, taking mechanism to pieces which they had no idea

Flora Thompson

how they were going to put together again. They made many mistakes, which passed undetected because the owners had no more knowledge than they had of the inside of 'the dratted thing', and they soon learned by experiment sufficient to enable them to put on a wise air of authority. Then the legend over the door was repainted, 'Motor Expert', and expert many of them became in a surprisingly short time, for they brought the endless patience and ingenuity of the craftsman to the new mechanism, plus his adaptable skill.

XIII

Growing Pains

But the holidays at Candleford only occupied a small part of Laura's year. At the end of a month or so a letter would come saying that school would begin on the following Monday and she had to return. Excepting the arrival of a new baby or two, or the settling of a stray swarm of bees on somebody's apple-tree, nothing ever seemed to have happened in the hamlet while she had been away. The neighbours would still be discussing the same topics. The crops were good, or 'but middling', according to the season. Someone had nearly a half-bushel more corn from their gleanings than the rest of the hamlet, and that was a mystery to others, who declared they had worked just as hard and spent even more hours afield. *'A bit of rick-pulling there, I'll warrant.'* After a dry summer the water in the wells would be dangerously low, but it had not given out yet, and, 'Please God, us shall get a nice drop of rain 'fore long. The time of year's getting on to when we may look for it.' 'Look for it! He! He! It'll come whether you looks for it or not. Nice weather for young ducks and mud up to y'r knees when you goes round to the well, *you'll* see, before you knows where *you* are.'

She found the hamlet unchanged every year; but, beyond the houses, everything had altered, for it was still summer when she went away and when she returned it was autumn. Along the hedgerows hips and haws and crab-apples were ripe and the ivory parchment flowers of the traveller's joy had become silver and silky. The last of the harvest had been carried and already the pale stubble was greening over. Soon the sheep would be turned into the fields to graze, then the ploughs would come and turn the earth brown once more.

At home, the plums on the front wall of the house were ripe and the warm, fruity smell of boiling jam drew all the wasps in the neighbourhood. Other jams, jellies, and pickles already stood on the pantry shelves. Big yellow vegetable marrows dangled from hooks, and ropes of onions and bunches of drying thyme and sage. The faggot pile was being replenished and the lamp was again lighted soon after tea.

For the first few days after her return the house would seem small and the hamlet bare, and she was inclined to give herself the airs of a returned traveller when telling of the places she had seen and the people she had met on her holiday. But that soon wore off and she slipped back into her own place again. The visits to Candleford were very pleasant and the conveniences of her cousins' home and their way of life had the charm of novelty; but the plain spotlessness of her own home, with few ornaments and no padding to obscure the homely outline, was good, too. She felt she belonged there.

Her freedom of the fields grew less every year, however, for, by the time her last year at school approached, her mother had five children. One little sister shared her bed and another slept in the same room; she had to go to bed very quietly in the dark, not to awaken them. In the day-time, out of school hours, the latest baby, a boy, had to be nursed indoors or taken out for his airing. These things, in themselves, were no hardship, for she adored the baby, and the little sisters, who held on, one on each side of the baby-carriage, were dears, one with brown eyes and a mop of golden curls, and the other a fat, solemn child with brown hair cut in a straight fringe across her forehead. But Laura could no longer read much indoors or roam where she would when out, for the baby-carriage had to be kept more or less to the roads and be pushed back punctually at baby's feeding-time. Her mother's bedtime stories were still a joy, although no longer told to Edmund and her, but to the younger children, for Laura loved to listen and to observe the effect each story had on her little sisters. She was also rather fond of correcting her mother when her memory went astray in telling the old familiar true stories, which did not add to her popularity, of which she had little enough already. She had come to what the hamlet called 'an ok'ard age, neither 'ooman nor child, when they oughter be shut up in a box for a year or two'.

At school about this time she made her first girl friend and wearied her mother by saying, 'Emily Rose does this,' 'Emily Rose does that,' and 'That is what Emily Rose says,' until she said she was sick of the sound of Emily Rose's name, and could not Laura talk about somebody else for a change?

Emily Rose was the only child of elderly parents who lived on the other side of the parish in a cottage like a picture on a Christmas card. It had the same diamond-paned windows and pointed thatched roof and the same mass of old-fashioned flowers around the door-way. There was even a winding footpath leading across a meadow to its rustic gate. Laura often wished she lived in such a house, away from interfering neighbours, and sometimes almost wished she was an only child like Emily Rose.

Emily Rose was a strong, sturdy little girl with faintly pink cheeks, wide blue eyes and a flaxen pigtail. Some pigtails in the school were as thin as rats' tails and others stuck out at an angle behind the head of the wearer, but Emily Rose's pigtail was thick as a rope and hung heavily to her waist, where it was finished off with a neat ribbon bow and a fluff of little loose curls. She had a way of drawing it up over her shoulder and stroking her cheek with this soft end, which Laura thought very captivating.

Her parents were in somewhat more comfortable circumstances than the hamlet folk; for not only had they but one child to keep, instead of the usual half-dozen or more, but her father, being a shepherd, had slightly higher wages and her mother took in needlework. So Emily Rose had pretty clothes to set off her flaxen pigtail, a pleasant, comfortable home, and the undivided affection of both parents. But, although she had the self-confidence of one who was seldom thwarted, Emily Rose was not a spoilt child. Nothing could have spoiled one of her calm, well-balanced, straight-forward disposition. Hers was one of those natures which are good all through, good-tempered, good-natured, and thorough in all they do; a little obstinate, perhaps, but, as they are usually obstinate with good cause, that also counts as a virtue.

Laura thought Emily Rose's bedroom was worthy of a princess, with its white walls scattered with tiny pink rosebuds, little white bed and frilly white window-curtains tied up with pink bows. There were no babies for her to nurse, and apparently no household tasks were expected of her. She could have read all day and in bed at night, if she had cared to, for her room was well apart from that of her parents. But she did not want to read; her delight was in needlework, at which she excelled, and in wading through brooks and climbing trees. Her way home from school skirted a wood, and she boasted that she had climbed every tree by the pathway at some time or other and this for her own pleasure, without spectators, not because she had been dared to do it.

At home she was petted and made much of. She was asked what she would like to eat, instead of being given whatever was on the table, and if the food she fancied were not forthcoming her mother was quite apologetic. But there were delicious things to eat at Cold Harbour. Once, when Laura called for Emily Rose during school holidays they had sponge fingers and cowslip wine, which Emily Rose poured out herself into real wine-glasses. On another of Laura's visits there was lambs' tail pie. The tails in the pie were those of still living lambs which had been cut off while their owners were still very young, because, Laura was told, if sheep were allowed to have long tails they would, in wet weather, become heavy with wet and mud and injure or irritate them. So the shepherd docked them and took the tails home to be made into a pie or gave bundles of them to friends as a great favour. Laura did not like the idea of eating the tails of live lambs; but it had to be done, for she had been told it was rude to leave anything at all, excepting bones or fruit stones, on one's plate.

At school, that last year, Emily Rose and Laura were known as Class I and had several advantages, although these did not include much education. They were trusted with the *Key* containing the answers to their sums and heard each other's spellings, or anything else that had to be committed to memory. This was partly because the schoolmistress, with all the other classes in the school on hand, had no time at all to devote to them; but also as a mark of her confidence. 'I know I can trust my big girls,' she would say. There were but the two of them and no boys at all in Class I. Most of the children who had been with Laura in the lower classes had by that time left school for work, or, having failed to pass their examinations, were being kept back in Standard IV to make another attempt at the next examination.

In summer the two 'big girls' were allowed to take out their lessons and do them under the lilac tree in the mistress's garden, and, in winter, they sat cosily by the fire in her cottage living-room, the condition attached to this latter privilege being that they kept up the fire and put on the potatoes to cook for her dinner at the appropriate time. Laura owed these advantages to Emily Rose. She was the show pupil of the school; good at every subject and exceptionally good at needlework. She was so good a needlewoman that she was trusted to make garments for the mistress's own wear, and perhaps that was the chief reason for their being given the freedom of the sitting-room, for Laura remembered her sitting with her feet on a hassock with yards and yards of white nainsook around her, putting thousands of tiny stitches into the nightdress she was feather-stitching, while Laura herself knelt before the fire toasting a kipper for the mistress's tea.

That picture remained with her because it was the day after St Valentine's Day, and Emily Rose was telling her about the valentine she had found awaiting her when she reached home the evening before. She had brought it to show Laura, pressed between cardboard and wrapped in layers of notepaper, all silver lace and silk-embroidered flowers, with the words:

> Roses are red
>   And violets blue,
> Carnations sweet,
>   And so are you,

and when Laura asked if she knew who had sent it, she pretended she had lost her needle and bent down to the floor, looking for it, and, when pressed again, told Laura that her kipper would never be cooked if she pointed it at the window, instead of at the fire.

The lessons set them by their kind but overworked mistress, learning long columns of spelling words, or of the names of towns, or countries, or of kings and queens, or sums to be worked out of which Laura had never grasped the rules, were a waste of time as far as she was concerned. The few scraps of knowledge she managed to pick up were gleaned from the school books, in which she read the history and geography portions so many times over that certain paragraphs remained with her, word for word, for life. There were stories of travel, too, and poems, and when these were exhausted there was the mistress's own bookshelf.

The lessons were soon finished; the long lists repeated to each other, parrot fashion; Emily Rose had done Laura's sums for her and Laura had written Emily Rose's essay for her to copy, and the spare hour or two was passed pleasantly enough over *Ministering Children*, or *Queechy*, or *The Wide, Wide World* or Laura would knit while Emily Rose sewed, for she liked knitting, and they would sit there, very cosily, while the fire flared up and the kettle sang on the hob and the school sounds came faint and subdued through the dividing wall.

During their last few months at school they had plenty to talk about, for Emily Rose was in love and Laura was her confidante. It was no childish fancy, she was really deeply in love, and it was one of those rare cases where first love was to lead to marriage and last a lifetime.

Her Norman was the son of their nearest neighbours, who lived about a mile from their cottage. On the evenings when Emily Rose stayed after school for choir practice he would meet her and they would walk through the wood arm in arm, like grown-up lovers. 'But you must only kiss me when we say good night, Norman,' said sensible little Emily Rose, 'because we are too young yet to be properly engaged.' She did not tell Laura what Norman said to that, or whether he always observed her rule about kissing; but when asked what they found to talk about her blue eyes opened wide and she said, 'Just about us,' as though there were no other possible subject.

They had made up their minds to marry when they were old enough and nothing on earth could have shaken that resolve; but, as it turned out, they met with no opposition. When, a year or two later, their respective parents discovered the state of things between them, they were at once asked to each other's houses as accepted lovers, and when Emily Rose went as an apprentice to a dressmaker in a neighbouring village she already wore a little gold ring with clasped hands on her finger and Norman came openly to fetch her home on dark evenings.

The last time Laura saw her she was as little changed as anything human could be after a decade. A little fuller of figure, perhaps, and with her flaxen hair wreathed in coils round her head instead of hanging in a pigtail, but with speedwell eyes as innocently candid and milk-and-rose complexion as fresh as ever. She had two lovely children in a perambulator, 'The very spit and moral of herself,' another stander-by assured her; and, according to the same observer, the kind, steady husband who stood by her side would not have let the wind blow upon her if he could have helped it. She was still the same Emily Rose, kind, straightforward and a little dictatorial; convinced that the world was a very nice place for well-behaved people.

Laura felt old and battered beside her, a sensation she enjoyed, for that was in the 'nineties, when youth loved to pose as world-weary and disillusioned, the sophisticated product of a dying century. Laura's friends away from the hamlet called themselves *fin de siècle* and their elders called them fast, although the fastness went no further than walking, hatless, over Hindhead at night in a gale, bawling Swinburne and Omar Khayyám to each other above the storm.

But the 'nineties were barely beginning when Laura left school and where she would be and what she would be doing when they ended she had no idea. For some months that was her great trouble, that, and the changed conditions at home and a growing sense of inability to fit herself into the scheme of things as she knew it.

Her mother, with five children to keep and care for, was hard-pressed, especially as she still insisted upon living up to her old standard of what she called 'seemliness'. Her idea of good house-keeping was that every corner of the house should be clean, clean sheets should be on the beds, clean clothes on every one of the seven bodies for which she was responsible, a good dinner on the table and a cake in the pantry for tea by noon every Sunday. She would sit up sewing till midnight and rise before daybreak to wash clothes. But she had her reward. She was passionately fond of little children, the younger and more helpless the better, and would talk by the hour in baby language to the infant in the cradle or upon her lap, pouring out love and lavishing endearments upon it. Often when Laura began speaking she would cut her short with a request to go and do something, or take no notice at all of what she said, not from deliberate unkindness, but simply because she had no thought to spare for her older children. At least, so it appeared to Laura.

Her mother told her in after years that she had been anxious about her at that time. She was outgrowing her strength, she thought, and was too quiet and had queer ideas and did not make friends of her own age, which she thought unnatural. Her future and that of Edmund were also causing her anxiety.

Her plans had not changed: Laura was to be a nurse and Edmund a carpenter; but the children themselves had changed. Edmund was the first to protest. He did not want to be a carpenter; he thought it was a very good trade for those who wanted one; but he didn't, he said firmly. 'But it is so respectable and the pay's good. Look at Mr Parker,' she urged, 'with his good business and nice house and even a top hat for funerals.'

But now it seemed that Edmund had no ambition to wear a top hat or to officiate at funerals. He did not want to be a carpenter at all, or a mason. He would not have minded being an engine-driver; but what he really wanted was to travel and see the world. That meant being a soldier, she said, and what was a soldier when his time had expired, regularly ruined for ordinary life, with his roving ideas and, more than likely, a taste for drink. Look at Tom Finch, as yellow as a guinea and eaten up with ague, putting in a day or two here and there on the land and but half alive, for you couldn't call it living, between one pension day and another. Even if he had been well he had no trade in his hands, and what was land work for a young chap, anyhow?

Then Edmund surprised and hurt her more than he had ever done in his life before. 'What's the matter with the land?' he asked. 'Folks have got to have food and somebody's got to grow it. The work's all right, too. I'd rather turn a good straight furrow any day than mess about making shavings in a carpenter's shop. If I can't be a soldier and go to India, I'll stop here and work on the land.' She cried a little at that; but afterwards cheered up and said he was too young to know his own mind. Boys did sometimes have these fancies. He'd come to his senses presently.

Laura's failure troubled her more because she was two years older than Edmund and the time was nearer when she would have to earn her own living. Perhaps she had had doubts about her vocation for some time and that was why she had seemed cold and reserved towards her. The situation came to a head one day when Laura was nursing the baby with a book in her hand and, absent-mindedly, put down the little hand which was trying to clutch her long hair.

'Laura, I'm sorry to say it, but I'm downright disappointed in you,' said her mother solemnly. 'I've been watching you for the last ten minutes with that little innocent on your lap and your head stuck in that nasty old book and not so much as one look at his pretty ways. (Didums, didums neglect him then, the little precious! Anybody who could read a book with you on their lap must have a heart of stone. Come to mum-mums, then. *She'll* not push your pretty pawdy away when you try to play with *her* hair!) No, it won't do, Laura. You'll never make a nurse, sorry as I am to say so. You're fond enough of the baby, I know, but you just haven't got the knack of nursing. A child'd grow up a perfect dummy if it had to depend upon you. You want to talk to them and play with them and keep them amused. There, don't cry. You are as you're made, I suppose. We shall have to think of something else for you to do. Perhaps I could get Cousin Rachel to take you as an apprentice to her dress-making. But, there, that's no good either, for your sewing's worse than your nursing. We shall have to see what turns up; but there's no denying it's a great disappointment to me, after having had the promise of a start for you and all.'

So there was Laura at thirteen with her life in ruins, not for the last time, but she grieved more over that than her later catastrophes, for she had not then experienced the rebound or learned that no beating is final while life lasts. It was not that she had particularly wanted to be a nurse. She had often wondered if she were suitable for the life. She loved children, but had she the necessary patience? She could keep the older ones amused, she knew; but she was nervous and clumsy with babies. It was the sense of defeat, of having been tried and found wanting, which crushed her.

There was also the question of what she could do for a living. She thought she would like to work on the land, like Edmund. It was long before the day of the land-girl; but a few of the older women in the hamlet worked in the fields. Laura wondered if the farmer would employ her. She was afraid not; and if he had been willing, her parents would not consent to it. But when she said this to Edmund, who had found her crying in the woodshed, he said, 'Why not?' Then, it appeared, he already had a plan. They would have a little house together and both work on the land; Laura could do the housework, for field-women's hours were shorter than those of the men; or perhaps Laura need not go out to work at all, but just stay at home and keep house as other women did for their husbands. They talked this over every time they were alone together and even chose their cottage and discussed their meals. Treacle tarts were to figure largely on their menu. But when at last they told their mother of their plan she was horrified. 'Don't either of you so much as mention such a silly idea again,' she said sternly, and 'for goodness' sake don't go telling anybody else. You haven't, have you? Then don't, unless you want to be thought mad; for mad it is, and I'm downright ashamed of you for such a low-down idea. You're going to get on in the world, if I have any say in it, and leave working on the land to them as can't do better for themselves. And not a word to your father about this. I haven't told him yet what Edmund said about working on the land, for I know he'd never allow it. And as to you, Laura, you're the eldest and ought to know better than to put such silly ideas into your brother's head.'

So that would not do; even Edmund was convinced of that, though he still said to Laura in private that he would not be apprenticed. 'I want to get about and see things,' he said, 'if it's only things growing.' Evidently the craftsman spirit of his ancestors on one side of the family had passed over his head to come out again in some future generation.

There was scarlet fever at Candleford that year and Laura did not go there for her usual holiday. Johnny came to stay with them instead, and did *not* bring the infection; he had been too carefully guarded. But he made one more in the already over-crowded home; although it must be said that he improved marvellously under her mother's firm rule. It was no longer 'Johnny, would you like this or that?' but 'Now, Johnny, my man, eat up your dinner or you'll be all behind when the next helping's given out.' The fine air and the simple food must have been good for him, for he put on weight and started to shoot up in height. Or perhaps his being there at the time of the turning-point of his health was a lucky accident for which Laura's mother got the credit.

All that winter Laura went on with her brooding. Then spring came and the bluebells were out and the chestnut candles and young bracken fronds were unrolling; but, for the first time since she could remember, she had no joy in such things. She sat one day on the low-hanging bough of a beech and looked at them all. 'Here I am,' she thought, 'and here are all these lovely things and I don't care for them a bit this year. There must be something the matter with me.'

There was. She was growing up, and growing up, as she feared, into a world that had no use for her. She carried this burden of care for months, not always conscious of it; sometimes she would forget, and in the reaction become noisy and boisterous; but it was always there, pressing down upon her, until the neighbours noticed her melancholy expression and said: 'That child looks regular hag-rid.'

This accumulated depression of months slid from her at last in a moment. She had run out into the fields one day in a pet and was standing on a small stone bridge looking down on brown running water flecked with cream-coloured foam. It was a dull November day with grey sky and mist. The little brook was scarcely more than a trench to drain the fields; but over-hanging it were thorn bushes with a lacework of leafless twigs; ivy had sent trails down the steep banks to dip in the stream, and from every thorn on the leafless twigs and from every point of the ivy leaves water hung in bright drops, like beads.

A flock of starlings had whirred up from the bushes at her approach and the *clip, clop* of a cart-horse's hoofs could be heard on the nearest road, but these were the only sounds. Of the hamlet, only a few hundred yards away, she could hear no sound, or see as much as a chimney-pot, walled in as she was by the mist.

Laura looked and looked again. The small scene, so commonplace and yet so lovely, delighted her. It was so near the homes of men and yet so far removed from their thoughts. The fresh green moss, the glistening ivy, and the reddish twigs with their sparkling drops seemed to have been made for her alone and the hurrying, foam-flecked water seemed to have some message for her. She felt suddenly uplifted. The things which had troubled her troubled her no more. She did not reason. She had already done plenty of reasoning. Too much, perhaps. She simply stood there and let it all sink in until she felt that her own small affairs did not matter. Whatever happened to her, this, and thousands of other such small, lovely sights would remain and people would come suddenly upon them and look and be glad.

A wave of pure happiness pervaded her being, and, although it soon receded, it carried away with it her burden of care. Her first reaction was to laugh aloud at herself. What a fool she had been to make so much of so little. There must be thousands like her who could see no place for themselves in the world, and here she had been, fretting herself and worrying others as if her case were unique. And, deeper down, beneath the surface of her being, was the feeling, rather than the knowledge, that her life's deepest joys would be found in such scenes as this.

XIV

Exit Laura

Her mother was stooping to take something out of the oven and as she looked down upon her, Laura noticed for the first time that her looks were changing. The blue eyes were bluer than ever, but the pink and white of her face was weathering. Her figure was hardening, too; slim young grace was turning to thin wiriness; and a few grey threads showed in her hair at the temples. Her mother was growing old, soon she would die, thought Laura with sudden compunction, and then how sorry she would be for giving her so much trouble.

But her mother, still on the right side of forty, did not think of herself as ageing and had no thought of dying for a good many more years to come. As it turned out, barely half of her life was over.

'Gracious, how you are shooting up!' she said cheerfully, as she rose and stretched herself. 'I shall soon have to stand tiptoe to tie your hair-ribbon. Have a potato cake? I found young Biddy had laid an egg this morning, her first and not very big, so I thought I'd make us a cake for tea of those cold potatoes in the pantry. A bit of sugar can always be spared. That's cheap enough.'

Laura ate the cake with great relish, for it was delicious, straight from the oven, and it was also a mark of her mother's favour; the little ones were not allowed to eat between meals.

Her father had put up a swing for the younger children in the wash-house. She could hear one of them now, crying, 'Higher! Higher!' Except for the baby, asleep in the cradle, her mother and she were alone in the room, which, on that dull day, was aglow with firelight. Her mother's pastry board and rolling-pin still stood on a white cloth on one end of the table, and the stew for dinner, mostly composed of vegetables, but very savoury-smelling, sim-mered upon the hob. She had a sudden impulse to tell her mother how much she loved her; but in the early 'teens such feelings cannot be put into words, and all she could do was to praise the potato cake.

But perhaps her look conveyed something of what she felt, for, that evening, her mother, after speaking of her own father, who had been dead three or four years, added: 'You are the only one I can talk to about him. Your father and he never got on together and the others were too young when he died to remember him. Lots of things happened before they were born that you'll always remember, so I shall always have somebody to talk to about the old times.'

From that day a new relationship was established and grew between them. Her mother was not kinder to Laura than she had been, for she had always been kindness itself, but she took her more into her confidence, and Laura was happy again.

But, as so often happens when two human beings have come to understand each other, they were soon to be parted. In the early spring a letter came from Candleford saying that Dorcas Lane wanted a learner for her Post Office work and thought Laura would do, if her parents were willing. Although she was not one for much gadding about, she said, it was irksome to be always tied to the house during Post Office hours. 'Not that I expect her to stay with me for ever,' she added. 'She'll want to do better for herself later on, and, when that time comes I'll speak to Head Office and we shall see what we shall see.'

So, one morning in May, Polly and the spring-cart drew up at the gate and Laura's little trunk, all new and shiny black with her initials in brass-headed nails, was hoisted into the back seat, and Laura in a new frock – grey cashmere with a white lace collar and the new leg-of-mutton sleeves – climbed up beside her father, who was taking a day off to drive Polly.

'Good-bye, Laura. Good-bye. Good-bye. Don't forget to write to me.'

'And to me, and address it to my very own self,' cried the little sisters.

'You be a good gal an' do what you're told an' you'll get on like a house afire,' called a kindly neighbour from her doorway.

'Wrap every penny stamp up in a smile,' advised the innkeeper, closing his double gates after Polly's exit.

As Polly trotted on, Laura turned to look across fields green with spring wheat to the huddle of grey cottages where she knew her mother was thinking about her, and tears came into her eyes.

Her father looked at her in surprise, then said kindly but grudgingly: 'Well, 'tis your home, such as it is, I suppose.'

Yes, with all its limitations, the hamlet was home to her. There she had spent her most impressionable years and, although she was never to live there again for more than a few weeks at a time, she would bear their imprint through life.

PENGUIN MODERN CLASSICS

LARK RISE
FLORA THOMPSON

Sensitive and book-loving Laura is born in the rural hamlet of Lark Rise, where life has followed an unchanging pattern for centuries and the days are governed by the rhythms of nature.

This is the unforgettable story of her beloved home: a place where children know the name of every bird, flower and tree; men work the fields; women gossip over the fence; and the last relics of country customs have yet to die out. Whether it is describing ancient traditions such as the Mayday garland procession, bringing the harvest home and singing ballads in the local inn, or introducing characters such as Laura's radical father, the pioneering Mrs Spicer, the eccentric bee-keeping Queenie and ladies who wear bustles to feed the pigs, this first part of Flora Thompson's autobiographical *Lark Rise to Candleford* trilogy captures a vanished corner of rural England and the timeless joys of childhood.

PENGUIN MODERN CLASSICS

CANDLEFORD GREEN
FLORA THOMPSON

Laura is now fourteen-and-a-half and setting off for a new life in the sleepy village of Candleford Green, as assistant to the clever, dapper Miss Dorcas Lane, who runs the Post Office.

In Candleford Green new ideas and new ways are coming in from the outside world, from Dorcas's famous telegraph machine to the scandalous sight of ladies riding bicycles. There are also new people entering Laura's life: the curmudgeonly old servant Zillah, the grand Sir Thomas, the Irish harvesters and the ardent young gamekeeper Philip White. As Laura adjusts to this world, the traditions and ways of her country childhood seem further and further away – and a different future beckons.

In this final part of Flora Thompson's charming and evocative *Lark Rise to Candleford* trilogy, the old finally gives way to the new.

PENGUIN MODERN CLASSICS

MAPP AND LUCIA
E. F. BENSON

'Enchanting ... even at their worst-behaved, his characters never stop being lovable' Philip Hensher

When the recently widowed Mrs Emmeline Lucas (Lucia to her friends) desires a change of scene, she determines on the picturesque seaside town of Tilling for an extended break. There, with her ever-faithful friend and accomplice Georgie Pillson in tow, she sets forth to wrest the reins of Tilling society from Miss Elizabeth Mapp. But the Machiavellian Lucia has not reckoned on the indomitable Mapp, who has no intention of giving up her supremacy. Has Lucia at last met her match?

Battle-lines are swiftly drawn as the ladies strive to outdo each other, using invitations to delightful garden parties and, above all, the recipe for 'Lobster *à la Riseholme*' as their deadly weapons (to the fascinated horror of their friends), for the position of doyenne of Tilling.

'We will pay anything for Lucia books' Noël Coward, Gertrude Lawrence, Nancy Mitford, W. H. Auden

With an Introduction by Philip Hensher

PENGUIN MODERN CLASSICS

THE GO-BETWEEN
L. P. HARTLEY

'Magical and disturbing' *Independent*

When one long, hot summer, young Leo is staying with a school-friend at Brandham Hall, he begins to act as a messenger between Ted, the farmer, and Marian, the beautiful young woman up at the hall. He becomes drawn deeper and deeper into their dangerous game of deceit and desire, until his role brings him to a shocking and premature revelation. The haunting story of a young boy's awakening into the secrets of the adult world, *The Go-Between* is also an unforgettable evocation of the boundaries of Edwardian society.

'On a first reading, it is a beautifully wrought description of a small boy's loss of innocence long ago. But, visited a second time, the knowledge of approaching, unavoidable tragedy makes it far more poignant and painful' *Express*

Edited with an Introduction and Notes by Douglas Brooks-Davies

PENGUIN MODERN CLASSICS

UNDER MILK WOOD
DYLAN THOMAS

'[Its] great strength is the Chaucerian life and liveliness of its sixty or more characters, enjoyed in all their spontaneous eccentricity' Walford Davies

As the inhabitants of Llareggub lie sleeping, their dreams and fantasies deliciously unfold. There is Captain Cat surrounded by fish that 'nibble him down to his wishbone', Mog Edwards, 'a draper mad with love' for shy dressmaker Miss Price, Organ Morgan, listening to the music in Coronation Street with 'spouses … honking like geese and the babies singing opera', while at the sea-end of town, Mr and Mrs Floyd lie in their bed 'side by side … like two old kippers in a box'. Waking up, their dreams turn to bustling activity as a new day begins.

In this classic modern pastoral, the 'dismays and rainbows' of the imagined seaside town become, within the cycle of one day, 'a greenleaved sermon on the innocence of men'.

Edited with an Introduction and Notes by Walford Davies

PENGUIN MODERN CLASSICS

BRIDESHEAD REVISITED
EVELYN WAUGH

'Lush and evocative ... the one Waugh which best expresses at once the
profundity of change and the indomitable endurance of the human spirit'
The Times

The most nostalgic and reflective of Evelyn Waugh's novels, *Brideshead Revisited*
looks back to the golden age before the Second World War. It tells the story of
Charles Ryder's infatuation with the Marchmains and the rapidly disappearing
world of privilege they inhabit. Enchanted first by Sebastian at Oxford, then by
his doomed Catholic family, in particular his remote sister, Julia, Charles comes
finally to recognize his spiritual and social distance from them.

PENGUIN MODERN CLASSICS

OFFICERS AND GENTLEMEN
EVELYN WAUGH

'A literary innovator, inventor of modern black comedy in the novel'
Malcolm Bradbury, *Mail on Sunday*

Guy Crouchback is now attached to a Commando unit undergoing training on
the Hebridean Isle of Mugg, where the whisky flows freely and HM forces have
to show proper respect for the omnipotent Laird. But the high comedy of Mugg
is followed by the bitterness of Crete – and the chaos and indignity of total
withdrawal or surrender.

Officers and Gentlemen is the second volume of Waugh's trilogy, *Sword of Honour*,
which chronicles the fortunes of Guy Crouchback. The first and third volumes, *Men
at Arms* and *Unconditional Surrender*, are also published in Penguin.

Penguin Modern Classics

THE POORHOUSE FAIR
JOHN UPDIKE

'A work of art' *The New York Times*

Published just four years after John Updike graduated from Harvard, *The Poorhouse Fair* is a brilliant allegory about charity. The setting is a poorhouse – repository of the old, the infirm, and the impoverished – on the day of the annual summer fair. The people are the vividly realized, unforgettable characters that only Updike can create. Short and succinct, *The Poorhouse Fair* speaks to those fears all of us have of growing not old, but dependent.

'A first novel of rare precision and real merit ... A rich poorhouse indeed' *Newsweek*

With a new afterword by John Updike

*Contemporary ... Provocative ... Outrageous ...
Prophetic ... Groundbreaking ... Funny ... Disturbing ...
Different ... Moving ... Revolutionary ... Inspiring ...
Subversive ... Life-changing ...*

What makes a modern classic?

At Penguin Classics our mission has always been to make the best
books ever written available to everyone. And that also means
constantly redefining and refreshing exactly what makes a 'classic'.
That's where Modern Classics come in. Since 1961 they have been an
organic, ever-growing and ever-evolving list of books from the last
hundred (or so) years that we believe will continue to be read over and
over again.

They could be books that have inspired political dissent, such as
Animal Farm. Some, like *Lolita* or *A Clockwork Orange,* may have
caused shock and outrage. Many have led to great films, from *In Cold
Blood* to *One Flew Over the Cuckoo's Nest*. They have broken down
barriers – whether social, sexual, or, in the case of *Ulysses*, the
boundaries of language itself. And they might – like *Goldfinger* or
Scoop – just be pure classic escapism. Whatever the reason, Penguin
Modern Classics continue to inspire, entertain and enlighten millions
of readers everywhere.

'No publisher has had more influence on reading habits than Penguin'
Independent

'Penguins provided a crash course in world literature'
Guardian

The best books ever written

PENGUIN (🐧) CLASSICS

SINCE 1946

Find out more at www.penguinclassics.com